STOLEN BY THE WIND DRAGON PRINCE

ARIA WINTER
JADE WALTZ

Purple Fall
Publishing

Publisher's Cataloging-in-Publication data

Names: Winter, Aria, author. | Waltz, Jade, author.

Title: Stolen by the wind dragon prince / Aria Winter & Jade Waltz.

Series: Elemental Dragon Warriors

Description: Purple Fall Publishing, 2020.

Identifiers: ISBN:

978-1-64253-392-7 (pbk.)

978-1-64253-208-1 (ebook)

978-1-64253-357-6 (audio)

Subjects: LCSH Space exploration--Fiction. | Human-alien encounters--Fiction. | Dragons--Fiction. | Shapeshifting--Fiction. | Science fiction. | Romance fiction. | BISAC FICTION / Science Fiction / Alien Contact | FICTION / Romance / Science Fiction | FICTION / Romance / Paranormal / Shifters

Classification: LCC PS3623 .I6675 S76 2020| DDC 813.6--dc23

Cover Design by Kim Cunningham of Atlantis Book Design

PRINTED IN THE UNITED STATES OF AMERICA

Dedication

To my husband: Thank you for all your love and support. You are not just my husband, you are my best friend and my rock. I love you more than anything.

-AW

To My Husband,
Thank you for being my support and rock during this writing journey.
I love you!
-Jade

CHAPTER 1

SKYE

Everything is chaos as alarms blare through the ship. Thomas runs ahead of me, the flashing red lights casting a pink glow over his golden hair as we race down the corridor. Smoke fills the hallways, so thick I can barely see the ground ahead. Disembodied cries and screams echo behind us.

My heart hammers as the sounds of blaster fire pierce the air. The aliens must have already forced their way in through the hatch.

"Don't look down, sis!" Thomas calls over his shoulder as he grips my hands firmly, pulling me along behind him. "We're almost to the escape pods."

Too late, I dart a glance at the floor. Bile rises in my throat at the dozens of burned, bloodied bodies haphazardly strewn around us.

An inhuman roar fills the air and a blast of light zings past my shoulder, hitting Thomas in the back of the head.

He crumples to the ground. The world slows as I drop to my knees beside him. Grasping his shoulder, I turn him toward me. His *eyes are open but unseeing. A broken sob escapes me as I pull his head into my lap.*

"No, Thomas." My voice is barely a whimper. "No."

～

I wake with a start. The fog of my nightmares slowly recedes as awareness trickles back into my mind. My gaze drifts to the flapping gray tarp in the gaping doorway, reminding me where I am.

I hate falling asleep. In my dreams, I relive Thomas's death every night.

"You're awake." Lilly leans over me and takes my hand. Her long red hair spills over her shoulders as she studies me in concern. "How are you feeling?"

Numb. "I feel fine," I lie and do my best to flash a convincing smile.

Her blue eyes narrow slightly. My best friend can always see right through me. "It gets easier, Skye. I promise it does."

I know that. I lost my parents three years ago to the flu that swept through our colony ships. Yet somehow, I never thought I'd lose my brother as well. He's only a year younger than me.

Tears sting my eyes but I blink them back as I correct myself. He *was* only a year younger than me.

Drawing in a deep breath, I lift my gaze to Lilly. "What's the plan for today?"

I pull the tarp aside to follow her out of the escape pod. The dry, desert wind is cool against my skin, a sharp contrast to the burning orange sun in the sky overhead. The scarlet sand stretches out in all directions. Wisps of dry dust sweep across the dunes, filling the air with the strange scent of spice, reminiscent of cinnamon and nutmeg.

What a coincidence to find such a familiar smell on this desert world.

"I'm going to go check out that area today," Lilly points off into the distance, toward the orange rock formations that rise from the endless sand. "If the soil is good there, we can plant some of the emergency seeds to establish a food supply. We might even be able to create a permanent settlement there. The towers and canyons should provide some protection in the event of a sandstorm."

"How do you know sandstorms will be an issue?" Milo asks.

I turn and he greets me with a pained smile. Milo is my friend and Talia's brother. He and Thomas are—I swallow thickly. They *were* the same age. They used to be practically inseparable on the ship.

Talia walks up beside him. "We don't know—it's just a guess. But it's better to be safe than sorry. Besides," she shrugs, "the escape pod is so busted up, it's only a temporary shelter until we find something more permanent."

A glance over my shoulder tells me that John doesn't agree. Even though I was part of the bridge crew as a communications and navigation specialist, we both trained as engineers, but it seems that only one of us has accepted that this strange planet is now our home. He knows as well as I do that the escape pods were only built for a one-way trip, and yet, he studies the control panel's bare electrical components as if he can fix it and send us back into space.

I roll my eyes. The pod won't even fly at this point, much less break the atmosphere.

I turn to Lilly. "Do you want me to go with you?"

She shakes her head. "Nah. I'll be fine. I'm taking the rover so I should be back soon."

I want to insist, but I know my best friend. She has obviously had a stressful week since we crashed. According

3

to the emergency protocol, her job as head of the Botany Department on the colony ships makes her our leader because no senior Bridge Crew officers were on our escape pod. Lilly complained to me just last night that she wanted, more than anything, some alone time to decompress. I think this little excursion will allow her the space she needs.

Each colony ship was equipped with several pods, capable of carrying sixty people each. I don't know how many pods escaped the ships after the pirates attacked. In all the chaos, our pod only launched a little less than half-full and I shudder to think of how many crew members may have been left behind.

We're hopeful that we'll link up with another escape pod out here but there's no way to tell where the others landed. The pod's computer is fried beyond repair, which is why I can't help but feel frustrated that John is still wasting time trying to make the damn thing fly.

"Shouldn't you at least take someone with you in case you run into trouble?" Talia asks.

Lilly pats the blaster on her hip. "I'm taking this with me. Besides, we've been here almost a week and haven't seen any predators or threats."

I haven't slept more than a few hours at a time since we crashed. My mind keeps replaying the nightmare of Thomas's death. So I'm too tired to argue that Talia's right; Lilly should probably take someone with her. My best friend is too stubborn to let me convince her of that.

Anna approaches, having overheard most of our conversation. She places her hands on her hips. "You shouldn't go alone. Take someone with you."

Lilly gestures toward the canyon. "But it's not that far. I'll be fine."

Anna shakes her head. "It's probably much farther than

you think it is. It's hard to gauge distance when the whole desert looks the same."

They argue back and forth for a bit, but as expected, Lilly wins out. A part of me is glad. As the one to make all the decisions, Lilly is under a lot of pressure and deserves a break.

We're not supposed to be here. We were supposed to find a planet with plentiful water and vegetation. But like it or not, this desert wasteland is now our home.

Argument won, Lilly hugs each of us in turn then she starts for the rover. She spins at the last second to flash me a grin. "Save me the spaghetti food pack for dinner, all right?"

I laugh and roll my eyes. I'm happy to grant her that because she's the only one who likes the spaghetti anyway. "I will," I promise. "Be careful."

I watch her drive into the desert, my gaze tracking the rover until it disappears from view.

Lilly has been missing for two days now. A sandstorm passed through the camp after she left, forcing us to huddle in the escape pod for shelter. For the millionth time, I curse this planet, wishing our colony ship had taken us to a habitable world, not some barren rock in the far reaches of the universe.

I shouldn't have let Lilly leave on her own, but she insisted. I just hope she was able to stay safe in the rover during the storm.

John thinks we should assume she's dead, but I can't do that. If she had died, surely, I would have known.

After all, I knew the moment my mother died. I felt her pass before I heard the news. The doctors reassured me multiple times that her death was quick and painless, but I never told anyone that I already knew. Only Lilliana knows my secret; she's the only one who would believe me.

No one believes me now when I tell them I know Lilliana's not dead. She can't be. Every instinct inside me screams she's still alive. And I'm not giving up until I find her.

Perhaps that's why I'm feeling eager behind the wheel of my rover and speeding like a madman across the red dunes. Out of the corner of my eye, I notice John's annoyed look. He's the one who insisted on accompanying me, but he's done nothing but complain ever since we set out.

As soon as we crest the next dune, my heart soars. A bright light in the distance—the silver glint of the metal frame of Lilly's rover—reflects like a shining beacon beneath the blazing sun. When we reach the light, I find the vehicle half-buried under the sand.

I practically leap out of our rover and begin digging with my bare hands, eager to find my friend. The fine, powdery red grains impede my progress. With each handful I rake away, another mound shifts and sand fills the gap again.

John eyes me, his hands on his hips and a hint of irritation in his gaze.

Frustrated, I jerk my head toward him. "Are you going to just stand there? Or are you going to help me?"

With a heavy sigh, he drops to his knees at my side and reluctantly starts digging.

Sweat beads across my brow as I dig furiously, hoping that Lilliana is still alive inside her rover.

She has to be. I can't bear the thought of finding her dead. I've already lost almost everyone I love; I can't lose anyone else.

A sandstorm passed through here. She's smart, so I'm sure she took shelter inside the cab. She's probably just passed out from the heat and exhaustion.

When we uncover the driver's side door, I jerk it open, only to find the cab empty. No sign of my best friend.

John places a hand on my shoulder with a sad look. "If she's not here, I hate to say it, but she is probably dead."

I don't want his pity. I shrug his hand away. "She's not dead, John."

He shakes his head, frustrated. "Look, I know she's your friend, but you have to face the facts. If she's not in the rover, there's no way she survived that storm."

"You don't know that," I snap.

He glances at the sky. "It's going to be dark soon. We need to head back to camp."

"Not yet." I scan the rover for any clues to my friend's fate. My heart sinks when I notice her blaster and jacket on the passenger floor. She wouldn't have left those behind unless she had no choice.

Tears sting my eyes and blur my vision as I stare out at the vast expanse of scarlet sand. Caught in the wind, sand grains weave through canyons and around the towering rock formations jutting up from the earth. I turn my gaze toward the pale-blue sky.

She can't be gone. She just can't.

Strong arms wrap around me as John pulls me into a hug. He gently runs a hand over my long, blonde hair. "I'm sorry, Skye. I really am."

Despite my resolve to remain strong, unbidden tears escape my lashes and run down my cheeks as I rest my head against his chest, struggling to hold back a sob. How could we have ventured so far into the dark void of space only for her life to end here? We could have forged a new life with the last of our people, escaping the world that generations before us poisoned beyond saving.

A soft scrape across my forehead pulls me back from my dark thoughts. John's chapped lips brush across my skin. He continues down my temple to my cheek and just as he's about to bring his mouth to mine, I jerk back, stunned. "What are you doing?"

"Just trying to offer you some comfort." He leans in to try again.

I place my palm firmly against his chest and push him away. "I'm fine."

He responds by tightening his arms around me. "No, you're not. You're in shock," he murmurs. "That's to be expected after losing a friend."

I shove him again. "Let go of me."

"Come on, Skye. I'm just trying to comfort you. Stop acting like you don't want me."

"I *don't* want you," I snap, staring incredulously.

His expression hardens. "What are you talking about? I've seen the way you look at me. We both know you want this."

Is he crazy? "I don't know what you're talking about, John. Now, let me go!"

He shoves me away, slamming me back against the rover. Pain explodes across the back of my skull as he cages me in with his arms. His towering form looms over me. "Stop playing hard to get, Skye. I'm getting tired of it."

John has always had a thing for me. But it's never been reciprocated; we're just friends and nothing more. In all the time we spent together on the ship, I've never had any reason to fear him until now.

"I'm not playing, John." I force myself to straighten and meet his eyes evenly, trying to appear unafraid so he won't think I'm weak. "I mean it! Let me go!"

He leans in to kiss me again. I knee him in the groin.

He yelps in pain, doubling over. I use the opportunity to escape.

"You're going to pay for that!" he snarls.

I dive into the rover, gripping the handle of Lilly's blaster

8

firmly before he jerks me back out by my ankles. My head hits the door as he slams me face-first against the panel. The world tilts and spins dizzyingly. He once again pins me against the frame with his larger form.

Using all my strength, I twist onto my back and jam the blaster's barrel into his chest. "Get off of me," I growl through gritted teeth. "Or I swear, I'll shoot you!"

A shadow passes overhead, blocking the light of the sun. Squinting toward the sky, I gasp when I see a hulking creature fly toward us.

Noticing my expression, John turns, following my gaze, and releases a shrill cry. "What the hell is that?"

A massive talon swipes out, throwing him off me. He hits a nearby boulder with a sickening thud before sliding to the ground in a crumpled heap.

I stare at the creature in wide-eyed shock. It's a light gray dragon straight from the old Earth legends, a myth made manifest before my eyes. It circles before landing in front of me. In a whirl of dust and wind, it transforms into a man covered in pale, gray scales that shimmer iridescently beneath the sun.

Stunned, I freeze as he reaches out to cup my cheek. His scales are unexpectedly soft against my skin. He studies me with a piercing gaze, his ice-blue, vertically slit pupils contracting and expanding as he stares down at me.

My head is still spinning and a part of me wonders if I'm stuck in a fever dream.

Tall, white horns spiral up from his head. My gaze travels over his face. He has a proud, square jaw and masculine bone structure. A long, jagged scar cuts from just above his left brow to the top of his cheek, and I wonder how he didn't lose his eye to this injury.

Instead of diminishing his beauty, the scar lends him a

dangerous, masculine edge. Not that I should be thinking about that while he eyes me like I'm his next meal.

He's taller than any human I've met and his shoulders are broad. His abdomen and chest are built with layers of rippling muscle. A strange, glowing pattern in the center of his chest draws my attention.

A soft laugh escapes me. I'm definitely dreaming. Dreaming of handsome alien dragon men in the desert— wow. That's a first for me.

He cocks his head to the side curiously and opens his mouth as if to speak, but only a low rumble escapes him.

I reach up to touch his arm. "I—I don't understand you," I barely manage as my head swims. I blink my eyes open and closed.

A deafening *boom* splits the air and the alien dragon-man jerks away, releasing a feral roar as he spins toward John.

Recovered, John stands with the blaster pointed directly at the alien. "How do you like that, you monster?"

The alien snarls, baring two large rows of fangs as he levels him with a dark, dangerous glare before shifting back into a massive dragon. He sweeps his tail into John, sending him flying backward.

The dragon spins to face me, carefully scooping me up into his clawed hand. A whirlwind of dust swirls around us as he flaps his massive wings, lifting us into the sky. Unable to stay conscious any longer, I close my eyes and surrender to my fever dream.

CHAPTER 2

RAIDYN

My mate! Mine!

The words ripple through me, suffusing body, mind, and soul as I take to the skies with my mate held firmly to my chest.

She is my fated one—my linaya. A glowing pattern swirls across the scales on my chest. There is no mistaking the fate mark. She is mine.

The fated bond is a gift from the Gods. As I look to my mate, I know I have been blessed for she is perfect in every way. With long silken hair the color of the sun's golden rays, piercing blue eyes that remind me of deep blue oceans, and soft, pale skin, my linaya is the most beautiful female I have ever seen.

I beat my wings furiously as I head back to Wind Clan territory. I feel as though I cannot fly fast enough. My mate has been injured and she needs a Healer.

I glance down once more at my chest. The fate bond swirls with a soft glow across my scales, directly between my two hearts. When I saw the bright light that fell from the sky toward the desert several nights ago, something inside me told me to investigate. Now, I realize why.

The impulse was a sign from the Gods that I would find my fated one. I send a silent prayer to them, begging them to help her survive while I curse Varus—the Fire Clan Prince and my former friend—for trying to hide these females from my people.

I saw him with a female who looked like mine only a day ago. Except her hair was the color of flame and mine has hair the color of the golden sun in the sky. I recognized the fated bond mark on Varus' chest as well, but he refused to tell me where he had found her.

This female appears to be of the same species as the one I saw with him. If he hadn't hoarded the alien females all for his Clan, my mate could have already been under the protection of mine days ago. I send another message of thanks to the Gods above that I found her when I did.

That disgusting creature was attacking her, and I shudder to think what could have happened if I had arrived any later. I have never seen such a creature in the desert. He smelled decidedly male, but was enveloped in a strong stench of filth, as if he had not bathed in several days. With a thick layer of coarse, brown fur covering his head, jaw, and lining his two beady eyes, he was a vile sight to behold.

I curse Varus again for withholding the existence of my mate and her people. She could have been violated by that male before I reached her. Even as this thought crosses my mind, I wonder where the rest of her Clan is. Where did they come from?

The trail of fire that marked the sky several days ago must not have been a meteorite, but rather a falling ship or escape pod. How else could this female have landed here? She is not native to this world.

Varus claimed the female he carried was his mate and his actions confirmed this was truth. He fought me as if worried I might try to steal her away, when I only was curious about her species and origins. He was so enraged by my approach, he would not even listen as I tried to ask him questions.

The last I heard, Varus was promised to the Water Clan Princess, cementing an alliance between their two Clans.

My father reached out to their Clan as well, but Noralla's parents rejected me offhand because of my scarred face.

I shouldn't have been surprised, but the rejection stung, nonetheless. One would think I would be used to such treatment by now. No female will have me, even with the promise of a royal title, because of my scar.

As I hold my mate tightly to my chest, I can only hope she doesn't feel the same. She did not look upon me with disgust when I first approached her. If anything, I noted a hint of curiosity and fascination in her expression when her sparkling blue eyes met mine.

Dipping my left wing, I turn and cross the border into Wind Clan territory. The desert beneath me gives way to green grass and tall trees. A thickly canopied forest scaling the mountains that loom in the distance.

My side aches, but I do my best to ignore the dull pain as we approach the castle. My mate's health is paramount; I need to get her to a Healer as soon as possible.

But the raw throbbing pain is agonizing and gnaws at my strength; I can feel myself weakening. Whatever weapon that creature used, it was powerful enough to pierce my scales.

My mate stirs softly in my clawed hand and my mouth drifts open when I realize I can sense her thoughts. They are muddled and slow at first as the fog begins to lift from her consciousness. She opens her eyes and releases a terrified scream.

"You are safe," I reassure her.

She freezes, then cautiously speaks. "Are you... talking to me?"

Despite my wound, a low chuckle rumbles deep in my chest. "Who else would I be talking to besides my fated mate? None but she could hear my thoughts as you do."

Surprise bursts through her mind and it occurs to me that perhaps mental communication between mates is not normal for her people. We are of different species, after all, and I did not truly consider the ramifications before now.

My suspicions are confirmed a moment later when she asks, "Fated mate?"

"Yes, you are mine," I tell her. "You are my linaya—my fated one—and I am yours."

CHAPTER 3

SKYE

"Yes, you are mine," he tells me. "You are my linaya—my fated one—and I am yours." His words are firm and absolute.

Fear fills me as I try to turn in his grasp but realize I can't move. Cold air whips my hair around me. I peek from the cage of his massive, clawed hand and my jaw drops as I spot his wings, fully extended like enormous sails in the wind.

I can't believe I was abducted by a dragon.

An involuntary scream rips from my throat and I grip him tightly. "Don't drop me!"

His body rumbles in what I assume is a laugh, quickly followed by his deep voice. "You are mine. I promise I will not drop you."

His? The memory of his sharp fangs flashes through my mind and panic snakes through my veins. He says I'm his, but what does that mean? Am I his slave? If so, I'd rather die fighting than live in a cage.

My gaze drifts over his massive, scaled form. Despite my fear, I beat at his hand because I have to do something. I'm not going quietly to whatever fate he has planned for me. "Put me down! Now!"

"You *want* me to drop you?" he asks incredulously. "When you just asked me not to? You would never survive a fall from this height. No," he huffs. "I will not let you go. It is not safe. You do not have any wings."

I open my mouth to argue but forget the words as I scan the ground rushing by below and realize just how high up we are. Lush green forests blanket the earth and winding rivers cut through the landscape. When I cast my gaze ahead, I gasp in wonder. Floating rock formations hang in the sky, like an image straight out of a fairytale. These islands suspended in the air are nothing short of breathtakingly beautiful.

They are covered in massive evergreen trees, reminiscent of the extinct sequoias on Earth. A waterfall drops off the side of the closest island, forming a pool on a smaller floating island below. Many are home to strange buildings made of intricately carved stone. Most of the floating masses of rock are connected by a thick mass of cables, covered in thick, winding green vines.

Several other dragons fly nearby, their scales various shades of white and gray. If I wasn't so terrified, I'd be overwhelmed by all this beauty. A fantastical landscape made of the vivid imaginings of an ethereal dream.

"You do not need to be afraid. I have you, my mate. I will care for you now," the dragon rumbles above me in low, deep tones.

"I'm not your mate," I protest. "You need to take me back to where you found me."

"You are mine," he growls in response, sending a small shiver of fear down my spine. "I will not take you back to that place. It is dangerous."

He's stronger than me and I realize I'm not going to win any arguments here. So, I'll just have to bide my time before I escape.

"You are wingless," he hisses. "You would be injured if you tried to escape. The fall from the city alone would most certainly kill you."

I still as panic joins the fright I feel. "You can read my thoughts?"

"Of course," he huffs. "I am your fated mate and you are mine."

Indignation burns through me. "I'm not yours. I don't belong to anyone."

"You are mine and I am yours. We are fated," he grumbles. "The Gods have ordained it. You are my linaya."

Before I can answer, he banks in a slow circle around a large courtyard below. My eyes widen when I notice a castle ahead. Light-gray and white stone walls are topped with triangular, peaked, dark-gray roofing. The architecture is reminiscent of images I've seen of ancient East Asian structures on Earth, and yet, this castle is unique to this strange world.

As soon as we touch down on the ground and he releases his grip, I run. I don't know where I'm going, but any distance from him is a win. A strong cord wraps around my waist, lifting me off the ground and yanking me back.

I scream and struggle against the rope only to look down and find that it's his tail. Digging my nails into his scales, I grit my teeth in frustration. They're hard as stone; I'm not even making a dent. He sets me down gently and relinquishes his hold on me. In a blink, he transforms back into a man.

A very naked dragon man.

I crane my neck to scan his impossibly tall form while he

studies me in return. When he opens his mouth to speak, only a rumbling growl escapes his lips.

"Where are we?"

He growls a string of syllables and I stare him down with a frown. "What are you saying? Why can't I understand you?"

He reaches for me and I bat his hand away, mildly shocked at my own bravado in the face of this hulking alien. I'm not about to go down easily. He thinks I'm his mate, and as my eyes drift down his massive form, I don't think I want to know exactly what that entails.

Covered from head to toe in light gray scales, thick ropes of corded muscle define his arms and legs. A long, whip-like tail curls behind him. Dark gray leathery wings spread out behind him. With broad shoulders tapering to a narrow waist, I can't see an ounce of fat on him. Sharp, black claws tip his five-fingered hands and toes. He has long, silken white hair that goes just past his shoulders. With a proud jaw, full lips, and aristocratic features, he looks like a marble sculpture of masculine perfection laced with a hint of lethal grace.

My jaw drops when I don't see the normal male anatomy below his waist. Instead, a long slit splits the scales of his crotch. I tear my gaze away from his form and meet his ice-blue eyes with all the confidence I can muster as he moves toward me.

Spreading my feet in a defensive stance, I raise my fists, readying to fight.

Dark blood drips down his side, pooling beside his left foot. I hadn't noticed it before, but now that I have, the memory of John shooting him with the blaster rushes through my mind.

He grips my forearm. Before I can hit his hand away, he speaks, "I must get you to the Healer and make sure you're all right."

I'm so thrown off-guard by his words that I nearly stumble back. Instead, I meet his concerned eyes. "Me?" I ask incredulously. "*You're* the one bleeding."

"My injuries can wait," he says. "Yours are more important."

CHAPTER 4

RAIDYN

My hearts clench as I stare down at my mate. She is strange in appearance, but beautiful nonetheless. How many times have I dreamed of finding my fated one? I can hardly believe she is standing before me. My gaze darts briefly to the castle behind her. I cannot wait to show her around our home.

She is smaller than a Drakarian female and lacks any sort of natural defenses from what I can see. With blunt claws, flat white teeth, smooth pale flesh instead of scales, she appears defenseless indeed. My protective instincts flare brightly as I look at her. And I want nothing more than to tug her to my side and fold my wing around her form, holding her close and keeping her safe from any and all danger.

Her blue eyes burn with fire. She may be smaller than the females of my species, but she is fierce and brave. When she struck me earlier, my chest swelled with pride. She does not seem to fear me anymore.

This is good. I will prove to her that I am a worthy mate.

Her gaze travels up and down my form appraisingly, lingering on the slit of my mating pouch. Perhaps she is already eager to claim me. But even as I think this, her eyes snap up to meet mine, traveling across my face and pausing at my scar. Does she find me appealing or hideous like most females of my race because of this disfigurement?

Flaring my nostrils, I scent the air. The acrid fear that covered her when I first rescued her from the offensive male in the desert has disappeared. Instead, I detect a delicate fragrance, unique and entirely hers.

I extend my wings to my side so that she may continue to appraise me, hoping she'll find me worthy to be her mate. The movement causes sharp pain to shoot through my side, but I force myself to remain still. I dare not show weakness to her. No female wants a male who is not strong enough to protect her and her fledglings.

I grit my teeth against the pain, reminding myself that my injury will eventually heal, whereas I might never recover from her rejection.

I move toward her, but she steps away, backing into the glass wall at the entrance of the palace. I place my palms on the glass on either side of her head and lean in, skimming the tip of my nose from her temple to her jaw and the curve of her neck. Gently rubbing my horns against her head, I inhale deeply of her rich and intoxicating scent.

She quivers slightly and I pull back, dismayed when her scent turns sour with fear. "What is wrong? I saved you. Why are you still afraid?"

She stares up at me silently, clenching her jaw. A tear slips down her cheek, but she quickly wipes it away as she holds my gaze.

When I reach out to cup her face, she jerks away.

"What is wrong?" I repeat.

She frowns. "Why can't I understand you?"

I blink, then grip her chin firmly in one hand to hold her still as I feel behind her ears, checking to see if her translator chip has been damaged. When I do not find one, I regard her curiously.

"You have lost your translator chip, but do not worry. I will make sure the Healer fits you with one, my mate. I will take care of you and protect you. My vow."

CHAPTER 5

SKYE

"**W**hy can I suddenly understand you?"

An irresistibly handsome smile curves his mouth. "This is how my people communicate with our fated mates—through touch." He pauses to take my hand. His scales are soft as silk and warm against my skin as he gently traces his thumb across my knuckles. "And since you lack a translator chip, this is the only way for you to understand me. In my draka form, I can hear your thoughts, as well."

"Your...draka form?"

"My larger form when I shift. The one that I carried you in."

I'm too stunned to pull away. My mind still struggling to process that he can shift forms into a real-life dragon.

He stares down at me in concern. "You need not fear me. I would sooner end my own life than hurt you. My vow."

"I..." I hesitate, unsure of how to answer. I want to believe him, but I have to ask. "What are you planning to do with me?"

He cocks his head to the side as if he finds my question strange. "Take care of you, of course."

I'm not sure how to respond to that, but at least I have more reassurance that he doesn't plan to harm me. "Why did you take me from my people?"

"That creature was part of your species?" he asks incredulously.

It takes me a moment to realize he's talking about John. "Yes."

He looks indignant. "But he attacked you."

"I—" I'm about to protest, but he's right. John did attack me. I shudder inwardly at the memory. I thought John was my friend, but it seems I was wrong.

"I guess I should thank you for saving me," I finally answer.

"You are my mate. I will allow no other to touch you." He growls menacingly. "He is lucky that I did not tear him apart for trying to harm my mate."

"About that," I mutter. "I don't understand why you think that I'm—"

He cuts me off with another handsome grin. "Your mate?"

I nod.

He thumps a closed fist to his chest. "I bear the fate mark between my hearts. Do you not feel it here? You are mine and I am yours."

It's obvious now that he won't harm me, but it seems we're still suffering from a serious case of miscommunication. So, I decide to start at the beginning.

I hold out my hand to him. "I'm Skye. What's your name?"

He stares at my hand for a moment before extending his. Lifting my hand to his lips, he places a tender kiss to the space between my thumb and forefinger. My lips part as my cheeks heat.

That was really romantic. Knight-in-shining-armor romantic.

His ice-blue eyes pierce mine. "I am Raidyn, Prince of the Wind Clan, and you are my princess."

My jaw drops. *Prince? Princess?* "What are you talking about?"

His arm extends in a grand, sweeping gesture toward our surroundings while he smiles at me. "This is our kingdom. And this," he motions to the beautiful castle behind me, "is our home."

The entire structure practically gleams beneath the light of the sun. The white stone walls are lined with several large windows. Thick, rope-like, green vines with glowing blue flowers climb the walls, casting an almost ethereal glow to the castle.

We're standing in a courtyard paved with cobbled white stones and surrounded by dozens of flowering plants with blooms of red, purple, blue and orange. It's beautiful here, but I need to get back to my people.

"I can't stay here," I shake my head emphatically and his expression falls. "I have to find my friend. She disappeared in the desert and—" I stop abruptly when I remember Raidyn's murderous intentions toward John. I open my mouth to speak, but the words won't come. Drawing in a deep breath, I steel my nerves. I need to know if Lilly is alive or dead.

"Raidyn, did you…" I pause, swallowing thickly against the bile threatening to rise in my throat. "Did you kill my friend?"

He blinks slowly. "What?"

"Did you kill another human? Like me?"

He shakes his head. "I would never kill a female."

My shoulders sag in relief and I release the breath I didn't realize I was holding. "Well, did you see another *female* like me out in the desert?"

He frowns and an angry growl rumbles his chest. "Yes. Varus, Prince of the Fire Clan, had her."

Simultaneously, hope and panic fill me. I hate the idea of Lilly being captured by a dragon, but if he Raidyn saw another woman, there's a chance she's still alive. "What did she look like?"

"Long hair the color of flame and pale skin dotted with several darker spots."

"That's her! That's Lilly!" I cry in excitement. But I quickly sober as panic moves through me. "This fire guy— Varus, you said—he wouldn't... eat her, right?"

He looks aghast at the idea. "Varus would never harm a female. None of my people would. Females are precious, treasured by my kind."

That's good to know. "Why is that?"

Sadness flits across his expression. "Several cycles ago, the Great Plague swept through our population, killing many of our females. Most who survived are barren. That is why our union is so special; the Gods have blessed us with the fated bond." He cups my cheek, brushing the soft pad of his thumb over my skin in a tender gesture.

Something touches my foot and I look down to find his tail wrapped around my ankle. He pulls me close while his tail snakes further up my leg, winding around my thigh.

I admit, it's not all that unpleasant.

Even as the thought enters my mind, I realize I need to get ahold of myself. I place a hand on his chest to gently push him away. "Wait a minute. What are you doing?" I glance down at his tail on my thigh.

His ice-blue eyes watch me with an emotion akin to long-ing. "I must touch you so we may speak. And I... never imag-ined the Gods would gift me with such a beautiful mate. My fated one. My linaya." He tips his head to the side. "You say your race is called human."

I nod.

He places a hand to his chest. "I am Drakarian, my beautiful Skye."

As he stares at me, I realize just how easy it would be to get lost in his eyes. The way he regards me and his tender words touch something deep inside me. Why am I feeling so flustered?

Softly, I shake my head as I push down my emotions. I've obviously read one too many romance novels. I need to focus on getting Lilliana back. "When you saw my friend with the fire guy, what was he doing with her?"

"He claimed she was his fated one," he replies matter-of-factly. His expression morphs into one of anger and a snarl escapes his throat.

"What's wrong?"

"I knew he was keeping secrets from me. If I had not found you when I did, you could have been hurt." He clenches his jaw. "I will never forgive him."

"We never saw your friend," I explain. "Lilliana disappeared from the site where you found me. But the fire guy never visited our camp."

He looks shocked. "He did not?"

I shake my head. "No."

"Then… he does not know the location of the remaining humans."

"Not unless Lilliana told him," I counter.

His expression darkens. "We must take a team of warriors to rescue your people from the Fire Clan territory and bring them here."

"Wait a minute," I shove his chest. "If he's part of the Fire Clan and that desert is his territory, what about you?"

He dips his chin in a subtle bow. "I am of the Wind Clan. This is our territory."

"So, the desert belongs to the Fire Clan," I mutter as I commit this information to memory. "And these floating islands are yours."

"Yes," he answers impatiently. "We must go get your people at once."

I meet his eyes evenly. "And what if I want to return to the desert and stay with my people instead?"

He frowns. "Why would you want that? We are fated, you and I."

A soft puff of air escapes me as I flash him a nervous grin. "That's... not how it works for humans. You seem like a nice guy, but I barely know you, Raidyn."

A smile quirks his lips. "What would you like to know? I will tell you everything."

He looks so earnest that his reaction would be endearing if he wasn't so stubborn as well.

"I'm sorry, Raidyn, but I'm not your mate."

"Yes, you are," he states firmly.

"No," I reply, equally as firm. "I am not."

"I do not understand why you are upset with me." His brow furrows softly. "Is it my scar?"

"Your scar?" I parrot as my gaze drifts over his face. "Why would I care about your scar?"

He blinks, taken by surprise. "My disfigurement does not bother you?"

"It's just a scar, Raidyn. But that's not the point. I don't belong to you."

"We belong to each other," he counters.

I cross my arms over my chest and glare up at him. "Shouldn't *I* have a say in that?"

He gives me a curious look. "What is there to say?"

"I refuse to be your prisoner."

He gestures again to his palace. "You are not a prisoner; you are my mate. You will enjoy all the freedom in the world. You are the Princess of the Wind Clan. This is your kingdom now, as much as it is mine."

"And what if I don't want to stay in Wind Clan territory?"

He frowns. "Why would you want to leave? Where do you want us to go if not here?"

Rolling my eyes, I huff out a frustrated breath. "*We're* not going anywhere," I gesture back and forth between us for emphasis. "But *I'm* going back to my people."

"You want me to return you to the desert and *abandon* you?" He stares at me in shock. "What kind of male do you think I am? I am not a dishonorable male. I would never abandon my mate."

I sigh heavily. This argument is getting me nowhere.

"Here." He grips my hand. "Let me show you our rooms. You can bathe and get clean. I will send for the Healer to fit you with a translator chip."

Mildly annoyed that he just implied I smell bad, I glare. "Shouldn't *you* see the Healer first?"

"Why?"

"You're injured." I point to his wound.

"Do not worry." He tips his chin up slightly. "I am strong and capable of protecting my mate."

Even as he brags, I note the slight sway in his stance as he straightens.

"You don't look so good, Raidyn."

He frowns. "I thought you did not care about my scar."

I place my hands on my hips. "I'm not talking about your scar. I'm talking about your injury. It needs to be tended."

"I am strong." He thumps his chest caveman-style. "Allow me to take care of you, my beautiful mate." He drops to his knees before me. "I vow that I will worship and protect you until I draw my last breath in this world."

I notice his scales have paled, which is a feat considering they were light gray already. He looks so sick, I'm worried he's about to make good on his promise of worshipping me as he draws his last breath, right here and now. His eyelids flutter open and closed as if he's struggling to remain conscious.

I grip his shoulders. "What's wrong? Are you all right?"

He meets my gaze evenly. "You must trust me." His words slur. "I will be well after a short rest. Please, do not leave. I promise to be a mate worthy of you, my Skye. I—"

His eyes roll to the back of his head and he slumps forward, collapsing at my feet.

Oh Stars, please, don't let him be dead.

CHAPTER 6

SKYE

I press my palms to his side wound, attempting to stem the bleeding as I cry for help.

How was Raidyn able to stand for so long with such a deep injury? Anger sweeps through me as I think of John. This is all his fault. If he hadn't tried to hurt me, Raidyn might never have intervened.

Another dragon-man rushes toward me. With dark-gray scales the color of stone and ice-blue eyes similar to Raidyn's, he ogles me. Glancing over my shoulder, he calls out in harsh, guttural tones.

Several more dragon men approach, each narrowing their eyes at me as they growl in warning.

Oh my Stars, do they think I hurt him?

I raise my bloody hands in a gesture of surrender. "This isn't what it looks like. I didn't hurt him, I swear; one of my people did. He thought Raidyn was a monster trying to eat me."

Judging by their hard expressions, they either don't believe my words or can't understand me.

"Can you understand me?" I ask the dark-gray alien, who nods. "Oh, thank goodness. That's a relief. Are you getting help for Raidyn?"

He nods again, but I note that his expression is still stony.

"Tell them to hurry. I think he's seriously hurt." I shake my head in frustration. "He tried to act like he was fine, but he's obviously not, and I—" I lift my gaze to the sky, trying to gather my thoughts. I tend to ramble when I'm nervous and I've never been more anxious before in my life.

"Raidyn says that I'm his—his mate." I stumble awkwardly over the words. "He says we're fated," I add, hoping one of these men can explain all this to me.

The dark-gray dragon lifts his wrist to his face and speaks into some sort of wristband. His language is a frantic stream of harsh syllables and tones I can't understand. Then he turns his sharp, furious gaze on me and begins speaking again.

"I don't understand you!" I tell him. "I don't have a translator chip. But I swear to you, I didn't hurt him."

He grabs my arm—gently, I note—and pulls me up to stand. He starts to lead me away from Raidyn, but I jerk my arm from his grasp. "Wait! I can't just leave him!"

I don't know why, but I feel strangely protective of this dragon-man I just met, who calls me his fated mate and regards me like I'm precious—the most precious thing in the world to him.

Yeah, I've definitely read one too many romance novels.

But I trust him more than these other guys. Despite touching him, I can't understand a word this dark-gray man is saying.

I yelp in surprise when he hauls me over his shoulder and starts for the castle.

"Wait!" I kick and scream in his hold. "I don't want to leave him!"

He bands his strong arm across the back of my legs, holding them still.

"Put me down!" I yell.

He keeps walking, giving me no indication that he's going to listen. So, out of desperation, I clamp my mouth around his wing joint as hard as I can, though my teeth don't even seem to make a dent.

However, that certainly gets his attention.

He hisses and jerks his wing from my grasp, then wraps his tail around my wrists, binding them together.

"What the hell?" I cry out. "Put me down! I'm innocent! I didn't hurt him! I'm his mate! I don't want to leave him!"

I'm hoping that if I keep telling them that I'm Raidyn's mate, they'll let me go. I can't help but be worried for him. At first, I thought he'd stolen me, but now I realize he thought he was saving me. And… he was. John would have probably raped me if not for him.

A horrible thought crosses my mind as the alien turns down a hallway with me slung over his shoulder. What if they're going to eat me? Now that Raidyn's down, who's to say these guys even care who or what I am?

Frantic, I struggle harder, desperate to escape. "Please don't eat me! My people taste terrible, I swear! We're—we're poisonous! You'll die if you try to eat me!"

The guard's shoulders shake, and I freeze.

Is he…? "Wait a minute. Are you *laughing* at me?"

Another guard joins him and the one holding me growls something to him. The new guy shakes his head and they both start chuckling.

Anger fills me. "Put me down right now," I push through gritted teeth. "Or I swear you'll regret it. When I get loose, you're going down."

They start guffawing, the guard beside my captor doubling over as he barks out another laugh.

That's it—these guards are jerks. Once Raidyn wakes up, I'm going to tell him everything and then these two jokers are definitely going to get demoted.

At the end of the long hallway, they step through a set of ornate doors. From my angle, I can't see the room, but I assume it must be massive since their footsteps echo loudly through the space.

The guard slings me forward and lightly places my feet on the floor. Despite his obvious attempt to treat me gently, I bat his hand away.

He stares gaping at me as if he cannot believe I've just hit him. He only has a moment to look stunned before both men drop to one knee, bowing in deference to someone behind me.

I still. The hair rises on the back of my neck as I slowly turn. My jaw drops when I come face-to-face with an older version of Raidyn.

This must be his father, the king.

Dressed in long, flowing, light-gray robes, he looks every bit as regal and aristocratic as his son. Right down to the stubborn set of his jaw as he glares at me.

One of the guards relays something and the king's eyes fly wide, then narrow as he turns his attention back to me. He leans in and grips my chin firmly, studying me like I'm a strange animal that just wandered into his home uninvited.

His lips pull back in a feral snarl that rumbles in his throat.

"You need to let me go," I tell him. "Raidyn says I'm his fated mate. He asked me not to leave him. I demand you take me back to him. Now."

He relinquishes his grip on my jaw, snapping at the guards.

They scramble to their feet and without warning, the dark-gray one slings me over his shoulder again. His tail wraps around my wrists and his arm encircles my legs, already anticipating that I'll struggle. Which I do. Excessively.

"Let me go!" I cry. "You'd better hope Raidyn never wakes up. Because when he does, I'm going to make sure you both get demoted. Or better yet—fired."

A chortled laugh escapes my captor.

"Yeah, laugh while you can, buddy. Soon, you'll be jobless. Good luck working anywhere after you get fired from the royal palace. How's that going to look on a résumé? I'll make sure everyone knows how you've treated me."

He stills and I wonder if he's finally taking my threats seriously.

Instead, he pushes through a large set of doors and we're plunged into almost total darkness as we start down another hallway. This one smaller than the last. Everything smells earthy and damp here. A cold breeze travels past us and I shiver. Whatever this place is, I already don't like it.

A moment later, he tugs me forward and lowers me gently to the ground.

Still incensed, I open my mouth to yell at him but stop abruptly when a force field drops between us. I'm so stunned, I reach out to touch it, only to jerk my hand away when it zaps me, hissing in pain.

What. The. Hell?

The guard sends me a pitying look as he mumbles something low in his throat.

"Wait a minute. What's going on? Why am I here? Is this a cell? Am I being locked up?"

An apology shines in his gaze. The other guard appears equally as upset, softly shaking his head. With a heavy sigh, one places his hand on the other's shoulder and they turn away.

"Wait!" I plead. "You can't just leave me here."

I glance around my cell, finding only a cot. Even more concerning than the lack of facilities are the bars directly opposite the energy barrier. It might be a lovely view if a sheer drop off the floating island wasn't waiting over the edge just on the other side of the bars. Raidyn's words replay in my mind: *You do not have any wings.* Yeah, wings would be helpful right now. Even if I could escape, there's no way for me to get off this island.

A forceful gust of wind blows through my cell as I watch a pair of wind dragons fly by outside. That's when it hits me —this cell is exposed to the elements. I could freeze to death in here if the temperature drops any lower.

How did I go from burning up in the desert to freezing in a cell all in one day? I hate this planet. I mean, I really, *really* hate it.

A soft noise draws my attention back to the force field. The guard has returned. As if reading my mind, he lowers the barrier just far enough to hand me a thick, furry white robe with an apologetic look on his face.

"Thank you." I manage a small smile. "Please, can you at least tell Raidyn when he wakes up that it wasn't my choice to leave him?" I shake my head softly. "He might have brought me here against my will, but he seems like a good guy. He saved me, you know. From one of my own kind."

Oh, here I go, rambling again. I really need to stop.

The guard's gaze holds mine for a moment before he bows. He turns and walks out, leaving me alone again.

CHAPTER 7

RAIDYN

Awareness slowly trickles back into my mind as warm air whispers across my scales, soothing away the deep ache in my side. A state of pure warmth and bliss suffuses me. All is right in the world. I have found my fated one and I cannot wait to hold her in my arms.

Extending my arm, I reach for Skye. When the tips of my fingers skate across silken scales, my brow furrows deeply. My mate does not have scales.

I open my eyes, jerking awake to find my personal guard, Tai, leaning over me. I pull my hand back from the dark-gray scales of his forearm.

Blue-green flames lick the surface of my wound as Healer Vonar breathes his healing fire across my injured flesh. I watch in wonder as the torn tissue slowly begins to knit back together. The healing abilities of my Earth Clan brethren are always a sight to behold.

He pauses, his eyes full of concern. "How are you feeling?"

I sit up, twisting slightly to test my wound, satisfied when the movement causes no pain. "Better," I reply. "Where is my mate?"

I glance around the med center, searching for Skye. I'm troubled when I do not see her.

"Who?" Vonar asks.

Tai seems hesitant.

"Where is the human, Skye? My mate?"

Tai mumbles under his breath, "She was telling the truth after all."

"What did you say?"

His eyes snap to mine and he quickly bows. When his gaze meets mine again, I read the panic etched into his features. "I—"

"Where is my fated one?" I growl low in my throat.

"We found her standing over you, covered in your blood, my prince. We didn't know what to do. When we questioned her, she did not understand and—"

"She does not have a translator chip," I snap. "Where is she?"

"Your father asked us to retrieve her—"

Alarm bursts through me. "My father?"

"Yes, my prince. He inspected her and believed she was lying about how you were injured. He ordered her locked in one of the cells."

My mouth drifts open in horror. The cells are dangerous for her. The nights have begun to turn colder here lately. Her skin is soft and fragile compared to the scales of my people. I doubt they offer much protection against the cold and the wind.

Panic spikes my blood and I jump up. I hiss as the sudden movement shoots a twinge of pain through my side.

"Take me to her," I command. "Now!"

Tai immediately turns and leads me toward the cells.

Behind us, Healer Vonar calls, "My prince, your wound is still—"

The rest of his words are lost in the wind as I follow Tai to my mate, praying to the Gods that no harm has befallen her.

"I'm sorry, my prince," Tai speaks hurriedly over his shoulder. "We did not know what to think when we found her beside your unconscious form."

"She is my fated one," I growl. "A gift from the Gods themselves. Besides, females are never to be treated so harshly. They are precious. Even if you'd found her drinking my blood like a cursed Mernin, you should not have thrown her in a cell like a criminal."

Worry mars his expression as we pause before the door to a long row of cells while he punches in the access code. "Forgive me, my prince."

I level him with a hard glare. "You should never have listened to my father. You know he hasn't been the same since my mother died."

He swallows thickly but says nothing.

Even as the accusation needles him, I realize this is as much my fault as his. Mother's death broke my father's mind and I should have challenged his rule long ago, taken my place as King to ensure peace and stability in the Wind Clan. But I did not have the heart to take anything more from my father. Not after all that he lost.

I curl my hands into fists at my side. "Pray she still lives."

For my sake, as well, I leave unspoken. I will never forgive myself if my mate suffers because I could not be the ruler my Clan needs. We all follow the rule of a broken leader even though I know it is wrong.

Tai shifts nervously, reentering the code to unlock the

hallway of cells. A sharp *beep* and red flashing light draws my attention to the panel as he frowns. "The code is not working."

Clenching my jaw, I turn my gaze in the direction of the throne room. My father is behind this, I know he is. A rumbling growl escapes my throat as I turn and start down the hallway. My father will pay for mistreating my mate. My vow.

"Where are you going?" Tai calls after me.

"To speak with my father." I flex my wings as I reach the prison's exit. I will reach him much faster by flying.

"But your injury, my prince—"

"I am not a fledgling!" I snarl. And it is time my father stopped treating me as such.

As I rush toward the throne room, the two guards stationed on either side of the doors barely have time to throw them open before I push my way inside.

Father's eyes snap up to meet mine, relief softening his features as he stands. He extends his arms and steps forward as if to embrace me. "Raidyn, my son. Thank the Gods you are well."

Although it pains me, I move away from his touch. My father loves me more than anything—he always has—but he has become overprotective since I am his only child and last connection to my mother. He loves me to the point of madness. I understand because I miss her too. But I cannot allow his all-consuming obsession with my health and safety to jeopardize my mate.

"Give me the code to the cells."

His gaze hardens. "No. That female claims one of her kind injured you. They are dangerous."

"She is my fated one, Father." I meet his eyes evenly. "You cannot keep her from me."

His mouth drifts open, dumbstruck. "Your fated one?"

I point to my chest. The glowing fate mark pattern swirls over my scales between my two hearts. "Yes. Now, give me the code."

He leans forward, his eyes wide and locked on the fated mark. "That fragile creature cannot be your mate."

I clench my jaw. "First, she is dangerous, and now, she is fragile. Which is it?"

Frustration burns through my veins as I read the indecision in his expression. My father was once a strong leader, decisive and confident. I see now that he is lost beyond recovery.

My gaze darts briefly to Tai, who has caught up to stand beside me. The warriors know my father's leadership is unreliable and secretly look to me for guidance. I finally realize that we cannot continue in this way. Only one male can be King, and it cannot be the one who occupies the throne in front of me now. Not when we have so much to lose to the Fire Clan if we do not act swiftly.

Instead of answering, he poses another question. "How were you injured? What kind of weapon could pierce your scales?"

"I was in the desert," I admit. "In Fire Clan territory when I rescued her."

His brows shoot up to his forehead. "You broke the treaty?"

I ignore his question. "I believe her people crashed in the desert. I saw a strange light falling from the sky not long ago. That is why I crossed into the Fire Clan lands to investigate. And when I found her, my mate was under attack by one of her kind—a male. I rescued her, but he shot me with an energy discharge weapon, similar to what the Elveron use. He thought *I* was trying to harm her."

"There are more?"

I nod. "Prince Varus of the Fire Clan had one with him.

He claimed she was his linaya as well. It was my mate's friend. She claimed this female was taken while scouting an area away from their crash site. We must find the rest of them before the Fire Clan does."

I point again to the mark on my chest. "This proves she is mine. And this also proves they are compatible with our people. The Gods would not have fated us if it were not so. Others might be blessed to find their fated among her kind, but we must reach them before the Fire Clan does. If they take them, our warriors will never have a chance to find out if they are fated to any other human females."

He shoots up from his chair. "Then we must free your mate so we can locate the rest. Before the Fire Clan do."

I blink several times. His moods and his decisions change so quickly, it is hard to keep up. At least for now, he is making sense. "Then, you approve of my mate?"

"I suppose I have no choice," he says grimly. "She does not appear to be strong, but the Gods do not make mistakes. They would not have paired her to you if she were as weak as she appears." He looks to Tai and the rest of our guards in the throne room. "We will organize a wing to find the rest of her kind in the desert. We will pair them with our strongest males."

My brow furrows deeply. "Pair them? You cannot force them to accept a male they do not choose."

My cousin, Durzain, steps from out of the shadows. "Is that not what the Fire Clan would do if they found the rest of the females first?"

I shake my head. Varus may be many things, but dishonorable is not one of them. "Prince Varus would never do this, nor would his parents, the King and Queen."

Durzain moves closer to my father and whispers in his ear.

I narrow my eyes. Durzain has always been favored by

my father because he is all that is left of my aunt—father's sister—after she died of the plague. But Durzain, unfortunately, is not an honorable male. I've told Father this, but he refuses to believe it.

And now, I wonder what Durzain is whispering in Father's ear.

Father's eyes turn to me. "Your cousin agrees with me. We should find the females and pair them with our strongest males. Who knows? If you have found your fated among them, there may be many others as you've suggested."

Durzain looks to me. "We will, of course, have to kill their males since they are so aggressive they are a danger even to their own kind, as you have witnessed for yourself."

With an imperceptible clench of my jaw, I address him firmly. "We cannot hold the rest accountable for the actions of one."

"No." Father slashes his arm in front of his chest. "They are dangerous. One of their males tried to kill you. I will not allow them to live if they are so dangerous. I won't risk your life, my son."

Frustration burns through me. "You think their females will be eager to bond with us if we start killing their people? If we force them to choose a mate before they are ready to even decide such a thing?"

Father and Durzain look at me but say nothing. They know I am right.

I continue. "We would never force a Drakarian female to make a choice. In our culture, the females choose when they are ready. They are not presented with several males and told they have to choose one right then. That is never how it is done, so why would we think it all right to do such a thing to the humans?"

Durzain scoffs. "I have seen your female. Unfortunately, their kind are weak. They should be grateful that our

45

warriors are even willing to bond with them and offer them protection. Why would they refuse something that is so obviously in their favor?"

I level an icy glare at him. "I will not stand by and allow this to happen. It is dishonorable and you know it." I turn to my father. "That you would even consider this shows me that you are no longer fit to rule our Clan."

A deep rumble rises in my father's chest. "I am King! You do not tell me what I can and cannot do. Now, go and retrieve your female. Bring her before me and we will organize a wing to locate the rest of the humans and bring them back here."

Durzain whispers in his ear again and Father looks to me. "Are you loyal to me or not?" he asks. "You are my son, and if you are to become heir, I must be able to trust you."

His words are a blade in my heart. Never has my father questioned my loyalty. Before this moment, I always knew without a doubt that he loved me above all else. Now, I realize that his madness has damaged not only his mind but his hearts as well. Durzain has taken advantage of this and poisoned him against me.

"I will bring my mate to you in the morning," I bow. "But first, I must make certain she is well rested and fed. Now, give me the code to the cells."

With a heavy sigh, Father gives me the sequence to free my mate.

Without another word, I turn and leave. I can hardly wait to free Skye from her cell. Anger fills me that she was even there in the first place, but I do not mention it now. No, I must make it seem as though I am going along with Father and Durzain's plans.

I will try to speak with Father alone later on, when Durzain is not around. If we are to bring the females here, it must be with the understanding that they have the same rights as our people. The females choose in their own time who they wish to take as mates. We should not present them with "eligible" males and then tell them that they must choose right then and there. That is simply not done and it should never be this way.

CHAPTER 8

SKYE

Desperate for warmth, I tuck my nose under the blanket. With my back to the wall and my legs pulled up to my chest, I'm wrapped in a cocoon of fabric, but I still feel ice cold in here. And the temperature is dropping now that the sun has set.

Who knew I'd be missing the desert after complaining all week about the blistering heat?

I wonder morosely what happened to Raidyn. To think I started to fall for his romantic words and near-poetic declarations. For a moment, I felt like I was living through a fantasy romance in real life. Except in this one, the prince and the dragon are one and the same.

Raidyn insisted that women were worshipped and treasured in his Clan, but as my gaze sweeps over what passes for my accommodations here, I'm pretty sure he was loopy from blood loss when he said so.

I'm reminded of the time Travis took me on a date and got drunk at dinner. He started spouting romantic lines about undying love. Luckily, I didn't sleep with him, because the next day, he didn't remember any of it. It had just been the alcohol talking.

My heart is heavy as my thoughts turn to my best friend. How could I have let Lilly go off on her own? I'd been so lost in grief over my brother that I wasn't thinking straight. I've been numb to the world since we crashed.

Part of me wished I had died with my brother, though I realize now, that was a product of the grief trying to take hold of me. I became lost in my sadness and that cost me my best friend. She's like a sister to me and I'll die if anything happens to her. I have to find her. I can't give up yet.

"Let me out of here!" I cry, my voice echoing through the cell. "Please!"

The only answer is the wind howling outside.

Talons scrape the floor behind me, followed by a low growl. I turn to find three dragon guys stomping toward me. I'm so cold, I can barely speak as I peel the blanket away from my frozen face. Although I can barely see anything through the darkness, I muster an indignant glare.

"If you're here to kill me, you should know I won't go down easily. So, do your worst," I grind out. I'm sure I would sound more convincing if my teeth weren't chattering so loudly.

One of the alien men rushes into the cells and drops to his knees before me. These guys have lethal claws and fangs. Despite my bravado only a second ago, I close my eyes, waiting for the death blow that I just know is coming.

He grasps my chin in a firm grip and my eyes fly open, finally recognizing Raidyn. Panic and concern are written across his features. "Are you hurt?" He pulls the blanket off my form. "Tell me."

I'm surprised at how happy I am to see that he's all right. But I can barely stand the cold. I grip the edge of the blanket tightly, trying to pull the fabric back around me. "I'm freezing to death." I smack at his hand, still angry that he brought me here in the first place and I'm about to die of hypothermia. "No thanks to you!"

He seems distraught as he wraps his arms around me. Tugging me close to his chest, he runs his hand over my hair. "You will not die, my mate. I will keep you warm. My vow." He spreads his wings to wrap them around me as well. He's so large that his massive form practically swallows mine.

And just like that, the romantic in me melts, both at his declaration and at the tenderness of his actions as he embraces me like I'm the most precious thing in the world to him.

At first, I consider struggling, but he's so warm and I've been so cold for the past few hours that I can't stop myself from nestling into his chest. He rests his chin on the top of my head and runs a hand reassuringly down my back. Almost immediately, I stop shivering as I curl into him.

"You're not going to let anyone kill me?" I whisper.

"No one will hurt you. I will not allow anyone to cause you harm." His voice is a low, soft rumble, comforting like a soothing balm over my panicked nerves. For some reason, I believe him. Though I don't understand why, he makes me feel safe, and right now I'm too exhausted to question the impulse.

He stands, lifting me against his chest. He carries me, bridal style, out of the cell and down the hallway as if I weigh nothing. It's only now that I notice one of the guards from earlier who brought me the blanket. The one with the dark gray scales. I look over at him. "Thanks for the blanket, but I still don't forgive you for locking me up."

Raidyn growls, glaring at the guard. "You are the one who imprisoned my mate, Tai?"

I make a mental note of his name. I'll make sure he's one of the first one to get demoted for throwing me in jail.

Tai answers in a string of unintelligible, harsh syllables, but I easily read the regret in his features. Seems he's worried about upsetting Raidyn. I actually feel sorry for him now—a little. I mean, he did laugh at me, and that was a jerk move.

"I told you you'd be in trouble," I tell him, then tap Raidyn's arm to get his attention. His sky-blue eyes turn to me. "If you want to fire him, fine. But nothing extreme like an execution, all right? After all, he did bring me this blanket."

Raidyn blinks, a hint of a smile quirking his lips, and the guard, Tai, releases a barking laugh followed by more words that I can't understand.

I narrow my eyes at Tai. "I wouldn't laugh if I were you, buddy. You're still on my bad list."

He laughs even louder, only stopping when Raidyn gives him a dark glare.

"Why can I only understand you?" I ask Raidyn.

"As I explained earlier, it is because you are my fated one. It is a part of the bond between us."

Fated one.

I remember him saying that before he collapsed. If that's what he thinks, I'm not going to question him yet. He just got me out of my cell, and I want to stay on his good side. Who knows? Maybe I can convince him to take me back to my people or help me find Lilliana.

It doesn't hurt that he's handsome—for an alien, that is. And he has vowed to worship and protect me, words that would make even the most stoic of romance heroines swoon.

"Do not worry, my fated one," he says. "I will get you a translator chip so that you can understand our language." He looks to the green dragon man on his other side. "Healer Vonar will install your translator when we reach your room."

I tense and stare up at him wide-eyed. "Are you talking about another prison cell?"

His wings tighten around me and he nuzzles my hair. "Never," he promises. "I will never allow anyone to put you in a cage ever again."

I'm about to ask for more reassurances but stop short when he opens a door to reveal one of the largest and most elaborately furnished rooms I've ever seen in my life.

This suite is fit for a queen in one of the books I used to read on the colony ship. A large, four-poster bed intricately carved from ash-gray wood is surrounded by a canopy of sheer white curtains. They blow softly in the breeze that drifts in from the balcony across the room. With a plush, king-size gray-and-white comforter, it looks so inviting I wish I could just fall onto the mattress and sink in.

A table and chairs carved of the same wood sit off to one side, on the gray carpets covering the stone floors. A deep impression in the far wall reminds me of a fireplace. Several tapestries line the walls, depicting dragon men both in humanoid and dragon form, surrounded by natural landscapes.

The room is breathtakingly beautiful.

My lips part as Raidyn carries me toward the bed. Panic grips me. Does he want to have sex? I haven't even come to terms with this fated bond thing yet. As he bends forward to lower me onto the comforter, I place a firm hand on his chest. "I—I've never done this before. I'm not ready to make this official yet, all right?"

His brow furrows. "We will not mate until you are ready. I am merely setting you down so that Healer Vonar can install your translator chip."

I glance to the side to find the green Healer dragon, Vonar, approaching me with what looks like a cross between a blaster and a syringe. Immediately, I start crawling backward, curling in on myself when my back hits the headboard.

Raidyn spins and growls at the Healer while his tail wraps around my ankle and halfway up my calf. Although I would never admit it, the touch is comforting somehow.

I grip Raidyn's arm. "You wouldn't let him hurt me, right?" I ask, watching Vonar warily.

He turns to me with a softer expression, cupping my face. "It will sting a moment, my mate. But that should be all."

My eyes widen. I have terrible pain tolerance. Desperate, I try to scramble away, but Vonar's hand whips out to wrap around my forearm and pull me toward him.

I scream out with panic.

Raidyn nearly loses control as he snarls and snaps at the man, who quickly backs away, both hands in the air in a gesture of surrender.

Vonar growls something unintelligible to Raidyn.

Raidyn's shoulders and head drop. He turns to me. "Do you want the translator?"

I blink. He's giving me a choice? Despite his reassuring words, I was still worried that I was a prisoner. On one hand, I hate the idea of pain, no matter how minimal, but on the other, it would be nice to understand the aliens without having to rely on Raidyn for translation.

Misreading my hesitance as a rejection, Raidyn's sends me a look somewhere between devotion and concern. "I do not mind translating for you, my mate," he whispers. "If you do not wish to wear a translator."

He really means it; he won't force me to get this device implanted. Touched, I reach out and take his hand. "Thank you," I murmur. "But I think I need one."

His gaze holds mine for a moment before he dips his chin in a subtle nod and then turns back to the Healer.

Vonar steps forward with the device that looks like an

instrument of torture, placing the injector behind my left ear. I grip Raidyn's hand tightly, gritting my teeth as I wait for the inevitable pain.

A sharp *click* behind my ear followed by a fiery sting makes me gasp. I tremble slightly, struggling not to cry out as the pain spreads across the back of my skull like fire. I double over, clenching my jaw as tears swim at the edge of my vision.

"What is wrong?" Raidyn snaps at Vonar. "Why is she still hurting?"

Vonar's mouth drifts open. "I—I do not know, my prince. I—"

The pain disappears as quickly as it started, and I lean back. Breathing a heavy sigh of relief, I rub the spot behind my ear. "The pain is gone. Thank goodness," I mumble to myself. For a moment, I was worried something had gone wrong.

Raidyn places two fingers under my chin, tipping my head up to meet his blue eyes. "You are well, my beloved?"

Despite the rational part of my brain insisting that I should be protesting his declarations of love and devotion, I find myself leaning into his touch as I give him a faint smile and nod. "I'm fine now. It still burns a bit, but it's getting better."

He turns to Vonar. "Give her your healing fire."

My brow furrows. "Healing... fire?"

"Yes. Vonar is of the Earth Clan, able to heal injuries and pain with healing fire."

He says this as if it's a logical, run-of-the-mill ability.

I tense as Vonar leans in, but I remain still, waiting to see what he'll do. If I know anything at this point, it's that Raidyn would not allow anyone to hurt me. So the fact that he's not flipping out right now means that I'm safe.

Vonar's warm breath whispers across my skin and the pain fades away to nothing.

When he pulls back, I reach behind my ear, pleasantly surprised when my touch doesn't hurt. "How did you do that?"

"It is our healing fire," he repeats patiently.

I turn to Raidyn. "Do all of you have this ability?"

He shakes his head. "Each Clan can breathe either frost fire or flame, but only the Earth Clan can heal with theirs."

As strange as it sounds, I don't question him further. All I want to know is what they plan to do with me now.

The Healer places his fist to his chest and bows slightly. "I am Healer Vonar."

"I'm Skye." Without thinking, I extend my hand to shake his but immediately recognize my mistake when Raidyn growls low in his throat behind me.

Eyes wide, Vonar backs away. "Forgive me, Sire," he tells Raidyn.

"Forgive him? For what?" I turn to face him.

Raidyn's voice is a low grumble as he stares daggers at the Healer. "For speaking to my mate."

"I can't speak to anyone now?" I ask incredulously.

He shakes his head firmly. "Not until we are properly mated. You cannot present yourself to him either. You are mine."

My brow furrows deeply. "Present myself?"

"As a potential mate," he replies. "You have already been claimed."

"Claimed?" My tone is indignant. "Like I'm some sort of possession?"

He tips his head to the side to regard me. "You are mine."

"Wait a minute." I shake my head. "I thought… you were giving me a choice." I gesture to the bed. "You said we didn't have to mate if I did not want to."

"Not until you are ready," he agrees.

"What if I'm never ready?"

"Do you not wish to be mine?" he asks as if the very idea shocks him to his core.

Before I can respond, Healer Vonar bows slightly, backing toward the doors. "I will leave you alone to talk." He disappears into the hallway.

CHAPTER 9

RAIDYN

"**W**hat if I don't want to be married?" she asks.

I cock my head to the side. This word translates as *bonded*, but surely she does not mean that. I feel I must ask anyway. "You... do not wish to be bonded?"

Her gaze travels up and down my form. "I—I barely know you. And we're not even the same species."

I do not understand. "What does that matter? We are fated to be together. Everything else is unimportant."

"Unimportant? Just how do you know we're supposed to be together?"

I place my closed fist to my chest, directly between my two beating hearts, watching in satisfaction as my scales begin to glow in the fated mate pattern beneath my touch. Her mouth drifts open as she ogles my chest. "This tells me you are mine and I am yours. The mark would not appear otherwise."

She kicks her leg out as if trying to shake my tail loose

from her calf. Afraid I have made her uncomfortable, I quickly retract it. "Look, I don't really understand what's going on here. You tell me that women are worshipped here, but I just got thrown in jail by a guy that looks like you but much older. Your father, I'm assuming?"

Ashamed at how she was treated, I lower my gaze. "Yes. He is the king."

"And you're the prince?"

I nod. "But my father is King in name only. The warriors have looked to me ever since my mother's death." Closing my eyes briefly against the grief, I continue. "My father has not been the same since she died."

A gentle touch to my forearm draws my attention. I find Skye staring up at me, something akin to sadness behind her blue eyes. "I'm sorry for your loss."

"Thank you," I reply softly. "She passed many cycles ago, but the deep ache of it still remains."

She turns her gaze to the opposite wall, seeming far away. "I know what it's like to lose someone you love. I'm sorry, Raidyn. I truly am."

Tears gather in the corner of her eyes, but she quickly blinks them away. My mate is no stranger to loss, and I wonder whom she grieves. However, I do not press her, because I understand how painful such memories can be when they surface. I will wait until she is ready to share that part of her past with me.

"Thank you," I reply.

A moment of silence settles between us and I glance around the room. I want to stay here with her, but she has said she does not wish to mate yet. So, perhaps I should sleep in the adjoining chambers. I am reluctant to leave because I worry that my father might order her imprisoned again if he suddenly changes his mind or is manipulated even further by my cousin Durzain.

She lifts her gaze to mine. "I need to get back to my people, Raidyn."

I have considered this as well. We must find her people, but as I think on the way that male attacked her, I am loath to return her to them. Especially now that I have her by my side and have vowed to protect her.

I frown. "But one of them tried to attack you. Are the other males dangerous to females like him?"

I hope they are not, and I pray what I witnessed was not typical of their mating practices. I know some species force-mate their females. The very thought sickens me.

"No, they are not," she replies. "And I appreciate your rescue, but I'm talking about the other women. My friends. I need to get back to them."

I shake my head. "No. It is too dangerous. If your own people are capable of attacking you, you are not safe among them."

Her mouth drifts open but she quickly snaps it shut. "No one has tried to hurt me but John. My friends would never—"

"If you do not know with utter certainty that the other males would not attempt to harm you, then it is not safe." I cross my arms over my chest. "I will not return you to such danger."

"Danger?" She spreads her arms wide in exasperation. "I've been in *danger* since the moment I got here. Your father had me thrown in a cell!"

She is right. As much as I dislike the idea of taking her back to her people, they must be warned. Even though I did not believe it at first, they would probably be better off with the Fire Clan. Even if Varus' people claim all of the females, at least I know they will treat them as if they were females of our own race. Not make them feel as if they must choose a male that is presented to them like Durzain has convinced my father we should do.

It may not be safe for us to remain here either. My cousin has my father's ear and I do not trust him. But neither is it safe for her to return to the desert—not without me, at least. She still has not deemed me a suitable mate. I believe she does not sense the bond as I do, and the mark has not manifested on her body.

She is mine, however—of this, I am sure. I must simply convince her to want me.

I meet her eyes evenly. "I will return you to your people," I watch as her beautiful face lights with joy, "but there is something I must share with you first."

Her brow furrows softly. "What is it?"

"Before I found you, I told you that I saw your friend with Prince Varus of the Fire Clan."

Something akin to hope flits across her expression. "Can you please take me to see her?"

With a slight clench of my jaw, I swallow thickly. "We are not on good terms with the Fire Clan," I reply haltingly, reluctant to tell the entire truth. Technically, we are now enemies, since I broke the treaty by attacking Varus in Fire Clan territory. "I believe that they may already be searching for your people to take them back to their capital city."

"Please." Her face is a mask of determination. "You have to take me to them. I have to find my friend; she's all I have left. I have to know that all my friends are safe."

"Varus claimed she was his mate. He even bore the mark that I wear now." I point proudly to my chest. "You need not fear. He would never harm her. And I do not believe that his people would harm yours, either."

She gives me a hesitant look. "This Varus guy... he wouldn't push her to mate with him, though, would he? Against her will?"

I jerk my head back, the mere idea twisting my stomach into a knot of disgust. "No," I deny vehemently. "None of my kind would ever force themselves upon a female to mate."

Unlike her kind, apparently, but I leave that part unspoken. After I witnessed the human male of her species trying to force himself on her, I understand why she would suspect other males of such a horrible crime. But Drakarians are not so evil.

My father and Durzain may try to force the females to *choose* a male to become theirs but they would never force a female to mate with someone against her will.

She releases a heavy sigh of relief then lifts her pleading gaze to me. "Please, Raidyn. Please. I need to see her."

Although we are not fully mated, I can already deny her nothing. If she wishes to be reunited with her people and see that they are well, I will do whatever I can to please her. "I must speak with my father about sending an ambassador to the Fire Clan. We cannot appear unannounced—they may attack us."

Her eyes go wide. "Attack you? Things are that bad between your Clans?"

I nod. "Unfortunately so."

I neglect to tell her that our relations deteriorated because of me—because I trespassed into Fire Clan territory to investigate what I thought was a meteorite that fell from the sky. And because I fought with Varus when he caught me. But as I study her, I realize any consequence is worth it. I have found my fated one and feel blessed beyond measure.

"Wait here. I will return shortly."

I move to leave, but her small hand alights on my forearm, stopping me in my tracks. I spin to face her hesitant eyes.

"Please, don't leave me here alone."

I cock my head to the side. "These are my rooms. No one will bother you here," I reassure her.

"Look, you're the only one here who cares about keeping me out of a cell. So, I'd rather not be separated from you while we're..." Her gaze travels over the room as if considering her words, "in your kingdom. All right?"

Part of me rejoices that she already trusts me to protect her and keep her safe, but another part hates that she views my palace and my Clan with fear. I want my lands to become her home if she will accept me as her mate.

With a clenched jaw, I nod. Father must accept her; there is no way around that. Surely, I can convince him to see reason. "All right. Let us go together."

She surprises me by entwining her arm with mine, as if already claiming me. We traverse the castle and I notice the not-so-discreet stares of several guards. No doubt word has already spread about my strange fated one. After all, there has never been a fated bond outside of our race before Varus and me. I glance over my shoulder at Tai, who trails us, and Skye narrows her eyes at him.

Though I regret that he placed her in a cell, I realize he had no choice. He could not defy my father's wishes, and I was unconscious at the time. He could have been punished for giving her the blanket and yet, he helped her anyway. Although I know she still harbors anger against him, Tai is a good male.

As soon as I walk into the throne room, my father smiles. His sharp gaze travels over Skye. "Do you know where we can find your people?" he asks.

Skye tenses beside me but says nothing. My nostrils flare as the acrid scent of her fear suffuses the air. I hate that she is afraid, especially of my father. Instinct drives me to pull her close to my side, draping one wing around her protectively as if to shield her from his piercing blue eyes as they rake over her form.

Despite her trepidation, she meets his eyes evenly. "What do you plan to do with my people once you've found them? Throw them in a cell, like you did me?"

He narrows his eyes. "I thought you were dangerous."

"And now?" she asks.

She is brave, my mate. Even though she is wary of my father, she still speaks her mind. I am blessed indeed that the Gods chose such a strong female to be mine.

My cousin steps forward. "Now, you will help us find your people. Once we bring them back here, they will be given a choice of the best of our warriors to bond with."

She frowns. "What if they don't want to bond with anyone yet?"

"Why would they not wish this?" Durzain asks. "They would be protected and—"

She narrows her eyes. "You make it sound like your offering us shelter and aid would mean we had to trade our freedom in return. Is that right?"

A low growl rumbles in his chest. "We do not condone slavery."

"Well, what you're offering my people certainly doesn't sound like true freedom," she counters.

"She is right," I tell them. "The females will feel as though they have to choose a male that we place before them. And—"

"Enough!" my father growls.

Durzain steps forward. "You will lead us to your people so that we may retrieve the females from the desert and bring them back here."

She shakes her head. "I'm not going to help you find my people. I don't trust you."

His brows shoot up to his forehead. "You do not trust us?"

he asks incredulously. "You and your people are the reason the prince," he gestures to me, "was so grievously injured earlier. Is that not right, my king?" he asks.

My father's eyes lock on hers and it is easy to see that Durzain's words are seeping into his mind. He is so lost, my father, and so easily swayed. I have known this, but never before now did I consider the danger of allowing him to remain in power until now that my cousin seeks to bend him to his will.

Father levels her with a menacing glare. "Durzain is right. Her people tried to kill you and yet she would question our intentions?"

Skye steps forward. "We thought he was attacking us. We—"

"Silence!" he snarls. He motions to one of the other guards. "Take her back to her cell while I decide her fate."

"You cannot!" I growl.

"I am King, not you," he pushes through gritted teeth. "I do this for you, my son. Can you not see that? Her people are a threat to our species."

"They are not—"

Cutting me off, my father turns to Tai. "Take her back to her cell. Now!"

Tai grimaces in apology and I growl low in my throat.

Without warning, I shift into my draka form and scoop Skye up with my claws.

She cries out in surprise as I race out the door and into the courtyard. Extending my wings, I beat them furiously to climb into the air, desperate to escape with my mate.

Behind me, Tai roars a battle cry. I turn to find him chasing me as we ascend through the clouds.

With my vision obscured, I call to him. "Do not pursue us! I don't want to hurt you, Tai, but I will if I have to! She is my fated one; I will allow no one to harm or imprison her!"

He pulls into line beside me and I spin, ready to fight.

"You should know better by now, my prince." He dips his chin in a subtle bow as his blue eyes meet mine. "I am merely giving chase as you head for the western border. I will report your last location to your father."

I grin, for I am heading south, and he knows it. Tai is not just my guard, but also my friend. He knows where I will head for shelter to hide my mate. "Thank you, my friend. May the winds guide you safely."

"And you as well," he replies, then circles back toward the castle.

Skye's small form trembles in my clawed hand.

"It is all right, my mate," I reassure her. "You are safe."

"Where are we going?"

"Far from here. To a place that my father will never think to look for us."

"Please, don't drop me." Her voice is tiny, barely a whisper. She probably believes I cannot hear her, and I suspect she has forgotten I can sense her thoughts through touch in this form.

"I promise I will not let you fall."

She stills. "You can really hear my thoughts while you're a dragon?"

"Yes," I confirm. "Can you sense mine?"

"No."

Her answer settles in my chest like a heavy stone. Why would the Gods gift us with the fate bond if she can neither feel nor understand its pull? Why does the fate bond mark not glow on her chest as it does on mine?

Perhaps this is a test. Perhaps I must prove that I am worthy of a fated one. Since my mate cannot recognize the bond and accept its pull, I must earn her love and prove to her that I am a good mate. I will do so gladly.

First, I must get her to safety. Away from my father and my cousin. I pray that Varus' people have already found hers.

Myriad thoughts float through her mind untethered as we soar through the sky. Images of her friend, the strange female with fire-red hair, fills her mind. Despite my attempts to reassure her, she worries about her friend.

But I suppose her anxiety is natural. This world and its people are new to my mate. She trusts me, but my cousin and father have made her wary of me as well. This knowledge is like bitter acid in my throat, but I resolve that I will change her mind. I will show her I am worthy of her trust and that I will do anything to keep her safe and happy.

We approach one of the floating islands along the southern border and a twinge of sadness plagues me as the house comes into view. This was my mother's favorite retreat when I was a child. We came here many times.

As far as I know, my father never visits the house. The memory of my mother is still too painful for him. That is why I know he would never think to search for me here. He does not know that I have returned to this island a handful of times since her death. I do not speak of my visits because we do not talk about her—ever. The loss is overwhelming, even after all these cycles.

The image of a strange young male floats to the surface of Skye's mind and my nostrils flare at an unfamiliar saline scent, reminding me of the vast oceans lining the Water Clan territory. I lift my head to study her and find that she is crying.

"What is wrong?"

"I was thinking of someone I lost." Her voice is full of pain. I wait for her to continue, but she falls silent.

An image of the male lying lifeless in her arms flits across her memories. Whoever he was, he is dead, and sadness overwhelms me that she grieves for him so deeply. "I don't want to talk about it," she finally whispers.

The image disappears, replaced by one of her friends again. I understand enough about grief that I will not push her for answers. When she is ready, she will tell me about this male whom she grieves.

Was he a friend? A relative? A lover?

The last thought should make me jealous, but I find that I am not. Whoever he is, she loved him greatly and I am sorry she suffered such a devastating loss.

CHAPTER 10

SKYE

Raidyn dips his wing to the left, banking in a long, slow arc over a floating island below. Covered in a forest of massive trees that rival images I've seen of the ancient sequoias on Earth, the landscape is wild and untamed compared to the other islands, which were covered with buildings and roads—signs of an advanced civilization. As we draw closer, I notice a small clearing with a house. Built to two stories, it looks like a rustic cabin made of the ashen wood of the surrounding trees.

This house could never be confused with the Earth cabins I've seen pictures of, however. With fine, silver metal accents and finishes, this structure is uniquely Drakarian.

Raidyn circles and then lands in a small courtyard in front. The house's entrance is picturesque, filled with various flowering plants with vibrant blooms in purple and pink. The flowers' shape is similar to roses, but larger and far more fragrant. A cool breeze sweeps in from the forest, carrying the smell of fresh rain laced with the delicate floral scent from the garden. The soft sunlight above does little to warm the chilly air but my robes provide enough warmth that I'm not uncomfortable.

Raidyn shifts into his humanoid form and I look up at him. "What is this place?"

"It was my mother's special retreat," he explains, and I note the strange catch in his voice. He told me she was dead; he must miss her. Dearly.

I understand his pain. I miss my parents every day. The ache has dulled over the past three years, but the hole in my chest was torn open again with the loss of my brother, Thomas.

Drawing in a deep breath, I push down my emotions as I scan the cabin before me. Surrounded by the towering forest and rich vegetation, this place is straight out of a fairytale. I glance at the woods around us, half-expecting a unicorn or fairy to step out from the shadows.

Despite all this beauty, I can't help but ask, "Are you sure we're safe here?"

He nods. "My father would never think to search for us in this place."

"Why?"

He hesitates a moment before replying, "This house is filled with too many memories."

When he doesn't speak again, I don't push him further. Instead, instinct tells me to take his hand. I may not understand the history behind his statement, but I can guess his mother is involved. I know enough of pain and grief to recognize its mark in someone else.

He turns to me with a questioning look and I give him my best attempt at a smile. "I'm sorry about your mom. I lost my parents, too. And thank you for saving me back there —again."

His expression softens as his ice-blue eyes meet mine.

"You are my mate—my linaya. You are the most important person in the world to me. I will protect you until I draw my last breath."

I want to protest that I haven't agreed to be his mate, but I hold my tongue. This man just defied his father and his king to keep me out of a cell. When he calls me his linaya, he says it with such pride, conviction, and, above all, passion. I know it's important to him, this fate bond he claims we share, but I... don't understand it. Not yet, at least. However, when he regards me with a softened expression full of love and devotion, I know that I'm willing to try.

And as my gaze travels down his nude form, I note again the absence of any familiar male anatomy, so there's that. I mean, how are we supposed to...

"You find me strange." Though his inflection doesn't change, I recognize the question behind his words.

"Well, a little bit," I admit as I allow my gaze to sweep over him once more. With his tall build, and strong, muscular form, he is nothing short of chiseled masculine perfection.

His scales shimmer with a pearlescent glow beneath the sun's rays. His ice-blue eyes search mine for a moment before he reaches down to cup my face, taking great care to retract his lethal black claws. Everything about him, from his tall, sweeping horns to his wings, claws, and fangs, screams *apex predator*. Yet when he regards me like I'm a rare and precious gift, I know in my heart he would never hurt me.

It would be so easy to let myself fall for him, but I'm afraid. He's almost too perfect and I worry that any moment now, he's going to realize he was wrong. That I'm not the woman he thinks I am and we're too different to be fated. There's still so much I don't know about him and his world.

With a heavy sigh, I lower my gaze again to the strange line that runs down his body where the typical human male anatomy would be.

"What is wrong?"

My eyes snap up to meet his. "Oh, um, nothing." My cheeks heat in embarrassment and I avert my gaze. "Your, um... male anatomy is... missing."

He's silent for so long, I wonder if he heard me. I look up to find him frowning in confusion. "Missing? You mean my stav?" He blinks several times. "Are you ready to mate with me already?"

My jaw drops. "What? No! I just—you look different from human men, and—"

"Ah," he says, understanding dawning across his face. "Your males must not have a mating pouch."

"A... *mating pouch?*" I ask. "What do you mean?"

He gestures to the long slit between his thighs. "My stav does not extend from my mating pouch until I am ready to mate. It is this way for the males of my species, but I know there are many species' males whose stav protrudes at all times."

"Yeah," I mumble. "Human men, uh... they *protrude* all the time. No pouch."

"Do not worry. My stav will emerge when you are ready to mate."

I send him a nervous smile. I'm curious what exactly his stav looks like because, depending upon what's inside his pouch, there's no guarantee we'd even fit together. But I know asking more questions might give him false hope, so I decide to wait on that particular concern. "Thanks. But—as I said—I might never be ready."

His expression falls.

For a second, guilt fills me.

I understand how it feels to yearn for something only to be disappointed. Yet he doesn't regard me with anger or uncertainty, but with devotion and hope for a brighter future... with me.

Instead of arguing that we're fated like he did earlier, he drops the conversation and gestures toward the entrance. "Allow me to show you around."

I'm excited to explore this place. All I remember of Earth is a tiny apartment in an overcrowded, smog-filled city with far more cement than trees or vegetation. This island is everything I used to read about ancient Earth and more. I always dreamed of staying in a real forest cabin.

I smile up at him. "All right."

He presses his palm to a panel next to the large, seamless metal door, which slides open. "Place your palm next to mine," he instructs, and when I do, a green light flashes around my imprint. He grins. "The house is now coded to recognize you. You may come and go as you please."

That would be more comforting if we weren't on a floating island. It's not like I can go anywhere, even if I leave the house. However, I appreciate his attempt to make me more comfortable. He swore I'd never be put in a cage again; this is his way of showing me that his word is good.

When we enter, my jaw drops. An enormous, gray stone fireplace takes up almost the entire wall. A row of floor-to-ceiling windows with a sliding glass door opens into a garden at the back of the house. There are dozens of flowering rose-like pink-and-purple plants, the same variety as the ones in the courtyard, and a stream winding through the backyard. The scene is inviting, as if beckoning us outside.

The spacious living area opens into what I assume is a kitchen, though I don't recognize anything beyond the typical countertop space; the appliances are all strange to me. Plush, floating sofas covered in rich gray-and-white fabric blend seamlessly with the dark stone floor and the massive stacked logs that make up the walls. This entire space feels both rustic and luxurious at the same time. A stack of wood lies in the hearth, making me excited at the mere thought of lighting a fire.

Massive gray wood beams span the ceiling. Off to the side, I notice a wide staircase that ascends to the second level.

He leads me up the stairs to find that the entire second floor seems to be one huge bedroom. A large four-poster bed with sheer green panels floats near the far wall. A table and chairs sit in the corner beside another fireplace. Despite all the intricately carved furnishings, my attention is drawn to the expansive balcony outside a set of sliding glass doors. It overlooks the garden, and from this vantage point, I'm able to appreciate the breathtaking beauty of the landscape below.

"Is there a bathroom?" I ask because that's the only amenity I haven't seen so far.

"Through those doors." He gestures to the far wall.

As soon as he opens them, I gasp. The space is palatial, to say the least. A large sunken tub in the center of the floor looks inviting, as does the shower encircled by a clear, rounded glass wall. However, I don't see a sink or a toilet.

"Where is the—" I start to ask but trail off as Raidyn pushes a glowing panel near the door. A sink slides out from one wall and what I'm assuming is a toilet slides out from the other.

I turn to him. "I'd like to get cleaned up."

"Would you like help bathing?"

My mouth drifts open, but I quickly snap it shut. Judging by the earnest expression on his face, he isn't flirting—he's trying to take care of me. "No, that's all right. I think I can manage by myself."

"But it is a male's duty to attend to his mate," he protests. "Every Drakarian male does this for his female."

"We're not mates, though," I gently remind him.

His expression dims, and he retreats into the bedroom. "If you need me, I will be out here."

I hate the sadness in his face every time I remind him I haven't accepted our bond. Whereas he's so utterly convinced that he already refers to me as his mate.

"Thanks," I reply as the door slides shut between us.

He truly is a sweet, handsome man, if I'm being honest with myself. But I'm still skeptical about his fated-mate claim. We only just met, and that was because he abducted me.

Well, technically he saved me, but I didn't know his intent at the time.

And now, here I am, developing feelings for him. I don't know what to do—or even what to think. I wish Lilliana were here so I could talk to her. She's always the first person with whom I share my problems.

I wonder if she's wishing the same thing right now.

We're both close with Talia and Anna, but Lilly and I are like sisters to one another. Stars, I miss her, and I hope she's safe with her alien dragon man.

Peeling away my clothes, I step into the bath and sigh in contentment as I sink beneath the warm water. All the muscles in my shoulders relax as I perch on the sunken ledge around the perimeter and tip my head back. A small basket near the edge holds what looks like several small bars of soap. When I pick one up and bring it to my nose, I smile. It's just as fragrant as the alien roses outside.

When I drop the bar into the water, it dissolves immediately, filling the entire tub with pink bubbles and the delicious floral scent. Allowing myself to float in the center of the large pool, I sigh again. This is absolute Heaven. I've never experienced a real bath before; I've had to take showers as far back as I can remember. Water has always been a luxury and heavily rationed, both on Earth and the colony ships.

When I close my eyes, Raidyn invades my thoughts. My mind replays images of his bare form, the embodiment of masculine perfection. Before today, I'd never seen a man naked outside of videos and images. Not that Raidyn is a man, per se, but close enough.

The way he wrapped his wing protectively around me in the throne room and then flew us off to safety was like a scene straight out of the many fantasy romance novels I used to read on the ship with Lilly. Except this time, the dragon saved the damsel instead of a human knight in shining armor. And now that I've experienced it in real life, I prefer the dragon version.

Would you like help bathing? His question resurfaces in my mind.

To be honest, I was tempted to say yes. I'm attracted to him, without a doubt. He's everything I would ever look for in a partner: kind, intelligent, handsome, and alpha-male protective.

I run my hands down my form, imagining they're his. The soap allows my fingers to glide sensually over my skin. There's something irresistible about him, those sharp claws, fangs, and horns, and that long tail and scar lending a lethal edge to his attractiveness.

I've never been wanted by a man before—not like this. Men have ogled me and asked me out, but I always knew they wanted only one thing: to spend the night with me. But my heart was fixed on forever, so I always turned them down.

The hopeless romantic in me waited for the knight in shining armor to appear and make me his forever. To proclaim his undying love and devotion, vowing to protect and defend me always.

Isn't that what Raidyn did when he called me his mate? His linaya? He wants me for eternity.

At the thought, I've never been so turned on in my entire life. Gently, I dip my fingers between my folds and find them already slick with arousal. I tease the partially hooded pearl of flesh at the apex and inhale sharply while an image of Raidyn touching me like this fills my mind.

I've touched myself before, but always in hurried motions, a rush to bring myself to a quick, brutal completion before my allotted shower time ran out on the ship. Here, I can take my time. Indulge in my fantasy as long as I want and—

A splash in the water startles me abruptly and I jerk up to find Raidyn in the pool with me.

"What are you doing?" I practically screech in alarm, trying to conceal my naked form beneath the bubbles.

"I tried knocking to check on you, but you did not answer. When I saw you floating, I thought something was wrong." His nostrils flare and then his ice-blue vertically slit pupils contract and expand as his expression heats. "I can scent your need," he rasps. "Are you entering your heat cycle?"

"My what?" I ask, alarmed that he not only scented what I was doing but has joined me in the tub, still naked and completely turned on, by the look on his face.

He inches closer, his eyes locked on mine. "Are you entering your heat cycle?" He clearly enunciates each word as if he thinks I did not hear his question before.

My entire body flushes with warmth. I swallow nervously because part of me wants to pull him closer even though I know I should be pushing him away. It would be so easy to reach for him. And why not? What's stopping me? Why am I hesitant to accept when he's offering me the eternal love I've always dreamed of?

His gaze holds mine for a beat before I lower my eyes. "My people don't have a heat cycle."

He stills. "But your scent—"

"I was just bathing." I quickly change the subject.

He nods. "Forgive me, then, for disturbing you. I will leave you alone."

When he turns to leave, pulling his body from the water, I'm afforded a view of his perfectly sculpted backside. His long, tapered tail only adds to the appeal.

I shake my head in a tiny movement, chastising myself for my errant thoughts. I hardly know this man. I need to get ahold of myself.

CHAPTER 11

RAIDYN

I curse myself inwardly as I leave the cleansing room. I am a fool. She probably believes I am treating her like a newly hatched fledgling. Drakarian females detest an overly protective male and judging by the look on Skye's face, I surmise human females feel the same.

It is difficult, however, because my every instinct demands I protect her. Especially while my father wants to imprison her again. I could have lost her to his madness when he had her thrown in a cell. She could have become ill, or even worse, she could have died if she'd stayed there, exposed to the elements any longer. Judging by the way she was shivering when I found her, I do not believe her species is able to regulate their body temperature as effectively as mine. I close my eyes as a small shudder runs through me. I could have lost my linaya in an instant, while I was unconscious and helpless to save her.

I struggle to leave her to her bath when every impulse

demands that I stay. I recognized the scent of her need in the cleansing room. I long to taste her sweet nectar on my tongue. The drive to mate with her, to claim her fully as mine, consumes me. My stav is engorged and presses insistently inside my mating pouch, desperate to seek the warm, wet heat of her center. But she is not ready to take me as her mate. I must wait for her decision.

What can I do to prove to her that I am a worthy mate?

With a heavy sigh of frustration, I head downstairs to take note of our supplies. I must make certain that my mate is well cared for while we are here, though I don't know how long that will be.

I cannot risk contacting Tai right now for fear that my father or cousin would intercept my message. I will have to wait at least a few days before I make the attempt. Right now, we are safe. If my father even suspected I was here, Tai would already have reached out to warn me.

I move to the kitchen. The stasis unit is fully stocked, so we should not want for food while we are here. Everything is in order, as it should be. I wonder when the caretakers were last here. They are only scheduled to come by a few times per cycle to make sure the house does not fall into disrepair.

My father never comes here anymore, and I only visit rarely, never for longer than a day. My father believes I find it as painful as he does to even think of this house and that I have stayed away as well.

Light footsteps at the top of the stairs draw my attention and I look up to find Skye staring down at me, dressed in the fresh robes I left outside the cleansing room door.

"I like it here," she murmurs as her gaze travels over the room. "But are you sure we're safe?"

This is not the first time she has voiced this concern. I hate the hunted look in her eyes as she asks yet again. I give her a faint smile as I struggle to push down the painful memories of my mother that this cabin brings to the surface.

"My father would never look for me here." She opens her mouth as if to object, but I interrupt. "Would you like something to eat?"

She smiles. "That sounds wonderful."

It doesn't take me long to prepare a meal from the stasis unit. I'm not sure what she likes, so I bring her a sample spread. It seems she prefers fruits and vegetables to the various meats I've lain out. Recalling her blunt teeth, I suppose it makes sense that humans prefer a vegetarian diet.

She lifts a piece of tavi fruit to her nose and delicately sniffs it. Cautiously, she takes a small bite and smiles. "This is amazing. What is this?"

"Tavi fruit," I explain, watching her devour piece after piece. Tavi is the preferred food of fledglings because it is easily chewed, but I do not tell her that. I am already hovering over her as if she were a fledgling. When she is finished with her second plate of food, I ask, "Would you like more?"

She shakes her head softly as she chews her final bite. Sitting back in her chair, she rests a palm over her abdomen. "I'm so full, I don't think I could eat anymore even if I wanted to."

She looks down at her hand. "On the ship, we were always rationing, you know. And sometimes, if there was an issue with the crops, I remember my mother used to give us her portions during those times, and still, we would be so hungry…" She trails off as her gaze drifts to the far wall, lost in the memory. "I think this is the first time I've eaten so much. I'm sorry."

I reach out and place my hand atop hers, resting on the table. "You do not need to apologize. We have plenty of food and you need not ration."

Her eyes snap up to meet mine. "Really?"

I nod. And at this moment, I vow that she will never know hunger again.

She turns her palm into mine and gently squeezes my hand. "I haven't thanked you for saving me... again."

"There is no need."

"Yes, there is, Raidyn. You defied your father. You're being hunted by your Clan because you helped me."

"It is nothing," I reassure her, because it is truth. Any Drakarian would do this for their mate. Especially their linaya.

"No, it's not," she denies firmly. Tears gather in the corner of her eyes. "I'm worried about you. What are you going to do?"

My brow furrows softly. She is worried about me? No Drakarian female would worry for a male unless he is her mate. It pleases me immensely that she is so concerned for me. Perhaps she does have feelings for me, despite her insistence that she does not wish to be my mate.

"I have given this much thought," I begin. "We will hide here for a while. Then we will go to the Fire Clan to find your friend."

Worry flashes in her eyes. "But I thought you were enemies. That it wasn't safe for you to enter their territory."

"Prince Varus and I were friends once." I sigh heavily as the memories return. "We used to be as close as brothers."

"What happened?"

"My mother and I were traveling through Fire Clan territory and were caught in a sandstorm." I swallow against the thick lump in my throat. "When the Fire Clan found us, my mother insisted they treat my injuries first, even though she was more severely wounded. She died that day." I curl my hand into a fist at my side. "They let her die."

Skye reaches for my other hand, her blue eyes piercing mine. "Your mother reminds me of mine," she says softly. "She must have loved you very much to insist that you be treated before her."

Tears swim at the edge of my vision as I lower my head. "She did."

"I wasn't there, but it seems she chose to risk her life to make sure you survived, Raidyn. It's a choice I think any parent would make. That's why the Fire Clan honored her wishes." A tear slips down her cheek. "My parents did the same for me, you know."

Shocked, I search her face, waiting for her to continue.

"Almost all of the colony crew was sick and there wasn't enough medicine." Her voice trembles. "My parents gave up their medicine to me and my younger brother. They loved us so much, they wanted to make sure we would live, Raidyn." I pause. "Several parents made the same choice, but not all of them died, like mine."

An image of the younger male lying lifeless in her arms flits through my thoughts and I suddenly realize whom she may have lost. "Your brother... is he among the other survivors?"

I already know the answer by the quiver in her bottom lip as tears stream down her cheeks. "No." Her voice is barely a whisper. "He was killed during the attack on our ship."

"My heart grieves with yours," I whisper. I gather her in my arms and she buries her face in my chest as her shoulders rack with suppressed sobs.

"The pirates who attacked your ship. Who were they?"

"I don't know. But they had scales like your people, and a long, tapered tail, sharp claws, and fangs. No wings, though."

Rage fills me when I realize what race she is describing. It is difficult, but I somehow manage to maintain a stoic expression. "I know of whom you speak—the Rovarans. It is fortunate that Varus found your friend and I found you."

"Why?"

"They are ruthless mercenaries and slavers. Your species resembles ones they covet, which would bring thousands of credits in the slave trade. It is highly probable they are still searching for your people."

Her eyes snap up to meet mine in alarm. "We need to go find the rest of my crew, Raidyn."

I move to reassure her. "I am certain by now that the Fire Clan has already discovered them and sheltered them in their capital city."

"How do you know?"

"Because that is what I would have done, if my father had agreed. Do not worry. The Fire Clan can defend against the pirates. We will find your friend. You will see her again. My vow."

She lifts her tear-filled gaze to me. "But it could be dangerous for you to enter Fire Clan territory. I don't want anything to happen to you."

If her expression was not so pained, I would be happy that she cares so deeply about my wellbeing. I run a hand gently over her long, golden hair. It is softer than I imagined, the fine silken strands slipping through my fingers. "I will be fine. Do not worry. We will wait for a few days and then cross the desert."

She nods and hugs me again.

Was ever a male blessed with such a caring mate? I think not. I used to pray the Gods would grant me a female who could see past the scar on my face, who would want me for *who* and not *what* I am. Now, they have gifted this female to me. They have blessed us with the fate bond. I now understand that the Gods gave me my scar so I could wait for the right female to accept me.

We sit on the balcony after consuming our meal, watching as the sun sinks low on the horizon. She gazes up at the star-filled sky.

"It's gorgeous here," she whispers, more to herself than to me.

A thought suddenly occurs to me and I stand. I extend my arm to her, offering my hand with a smile. "I would like to show you something."

Cautiously, she takes my hand. "What is it?"

I arch a brow. "Do you trust me?"

She grins. "If you had asked me that only a day ago, I would have said no, but now? Yes, I do."

My heart swells at her words. Trust is vital between a mated pair. I never imagined I'd earn hers so soon.

I place an arm behind her back and sling the other under her knees to lift her to my chest. My heart stops as a stunning smile curves her lips and she wraps her arms around my neck. "What are you doing?"

"We're going to fly."

She blinks. "But I thought you had to shift into your other form."

I shake my head. "No, I am perfectly capable of flying like this. I simply prefer the other form." What I do not tell her is that I prefer this form because I can hold her in my arms, close to my chest.

I move to the edge of the balcony and she grips me tighter. "Are you ready?"

She nods and I step off the ledge. She yelps in surprise as I extend my wings to catch the air, flapping furiously to climb above the tree line. I slip into an air current and glide toward the larger floating island nearby so she can inspect the city below.

It is nighttime. Most have already returned to their homes. Those who have not, pay us no mind, as I've made sure her robe covers her form, concealing her alien features.

She stares wide-eyed at the city. It is not as large as the capital, but still impressive by any standard. Tall buildings carved from light-gray and white stone shimmer softly beneath the light of the moon overhead. Water spills over the edge of the smaller island above, feeding the small river that winds through the city center before it, too, drops off the side into another smaller island that holds an extension of the city. The white mist of the waterfall appears like smoke dissolving into the sky.

Long vines trail down the side of the buildings, their verdant shades a beautiful contrast to the grayscale stone. The wonder in my mate's eyes makes me view the city through an entirely different lens, marveling at its beauty in a way I never have before.

"Can you go higher?" she asks.

I smile and then slip into another current, spiraling up toward the clouds. As we ascend, she studies the stars in awe.

"This is beautiful, Raidyn."

As I regard my perfect mate in my arms, I could not agree more. She is the loveliest thing I have ever seen and I am honored the Gods fated me to this glorious female.

When we return to the house, I set us down gently on the balcony. She steps out of my arms and already, I miss the press of her body against mine.

"I love it here, Raidyn," she murmurs. "It's so peaceful. Like the perfect getaway from everything else."

"I have always considered this a sanctuary," I tell her. "I am glad that you like it, for it is just as much yours as it is mine."

She lowers her gaze and I can see the indecision that wars

inside her. She cares for me—of this, I am certain. But she is still unsure if she desires to be my mate.

I am a patient male. The Gods did not gift us the fated bond without reason. I am already hers and I vow that some day, she will become mine as well.

CHAPTER 12

SKYE

Flying with Raidyn was amazing. Sharing this house with him... it's like a beautiful dream. I never imagined such a sanctuary existed. The moon casts enough light that I'm able to navigate the small path through the gardens easily.

Raidyn leads me through the rose-like blossoming plants, explaining the meaning behind each variation and color. "This one," he points to one with vibrant deep blue petals, "was a gift to my mother from the Water Clan after the signing of our treaty. And this one," he points to a triangular red blossom striped with orange, "was a gift from Varus' parents—the King and Queen of the Fire Clan—when we allied with their people."

"Is that normal?" I ask. "To gift plants?"

He studies me for a moment as if my question were strange. "Of course. Life is precious. To gift a living thing holds great meaning."

What a beautiful philosophy, to hold life in such high

regard, when most humans would consider a plant a simple gift. It is humbling, in a way, that Raidyn's people place life above gems and precious metals.

The bubbling sound of running water drifts throughout the garden. A small waterfall spills over a rock formation in the far corner, feeding into a winding stream and ending in a pond near the back of the house. This garden feels almost magical, pulled from the illustrated pages of every fairytale book I read as a child.

I don't even realize I'm holding onto his arm until he reaches out to pick a flower for me. Its petals are a light cobalt blue and I gasp, transfixed, when the bloom expands in my hand, releasing its delicate fragrance. "This is beautiful."

His gaze holds mine as he gently tucks a stray tendril of hair behind my ear. "It matches the color of your eyes."

My face heats with warmth under his scrutiny. He touches his fingers lightly to my cheek, leaving a trail of fire in their wake as he studies me intently.

"Your coloring," he murmurs. "It has changed to a deeper shade of pink. Almost red." He tips his head to the side. "What does this mean?"

Slightly nervous, I lower my eyes. "When humans do this, it means we are nervous or excited or," I swallow thickly, "attracted to someone."

He stills. "And... which are you now?"

I'm attracted to him. How could I not be? But I'm not ready to admit it just yet. I still haven't worked through the rest of my emotions. I already know he wants me forever, but forever is a long time. And we've only recently met. My heart is aching to fall, but my head keeps insisting on caution.

Instead of answering, I change the subject, thinking back

on all my romance novels. The very reasons I'm finding him so hard to resist. "Do Drakarians like to read?"

His lips quirk up at the edges and he leads me inside. A set of doors next to the kitchen opens to reveal a room I didn't notice before. Scrolls line the walls of the room—a library just like the ones in ancient Earth history.

I'm surprised such a technologically advanced species stores information on parchment rather than electronically. I give him a curious look. "Your people keep records on scrolls?"

He laughs. "You make us sound primitive." Shaking his head, he pulls a scroll from a nearby shelf. When he unrolls it on the large table in the center of the room, my jaw drops. A digital display scrolls across the parchment. He waves his hand over the screen and then flicks his wrist, causing the image to float in front of us.

Crossing his arms over his chest, he arches a condescending brow.

I roll my eyes. "I wasn't suggesting your people were primitive. I was just surprised, that's all."

The small smirk that twists his lips tells me he isn't entirely convinced. "All of the information contained on these is easily accessible in a universal database," he explains. "But my mother was sentimental and liked to have personal copies of everything she enjoyed reading. That is why all of these are here."

I turn my attention back to the floating display and my expression falls. Strange glyphs and myriad symbols fill the screen. I can't read any of it.

He senses my despair. "What is wrong?"

"I can't make out this writing. And I love to read. I was just hoping that I could—"

He takes my hand in his and flicks our joined wrists at the

display. Suddenly, the writing morphs into Earth Common. I blink several times, awestruck. "How did you do that?"

"If you want your translator to display writing in your language, you must simply wave your hand, like so." He demonstrates with his free hand.

A gasp escapes me as I scan the display, softy biting my lower lip as I begin to read. A smile crests my lips. "This is fiction?"

He nods. "My mother was very fond of imaginative stories of romance and adventure."

"So am I." I allow my gaze to drift over the other scrolls in the room, excited at the possibility of so many new books to read. All of them created by an alien civilization, no less.

As if anticipating my next question, he says, "Almost all of these are fictional stories. You are welcome to read them all, if you like, and take some with you when we leave."

I reach out and rest my hand on one of the scrolls reverently. I can hardly contain my joy. Reading has always been so important to me. Finding a familiar comfort in an alien world is more than I could ever have asked for. Without thinking, I turn toward him and stretch up on my toes. I twine my arms around his neck and hug him tightly. "Thank you, Raidyn. This is amazing."

When I pull back, I find his gaze heated and my cheeks flush with warmth once more.

"Your skin has changed colors again. What does this mean?" His lips curve in a small smile and I suspect he knows exactly what it means.

I lower my eyes, unwilling to answer. Instead, I change the subject again. "It's getting late. Where will we sleep?"

He tips his head to the side. "The bed, of course. Where else?" His brows knit together. "Unless your people prefer to sleep outside?"

My mouth drifts open but I quickly snap it shut. I realize

I should probably insist he take the couch, but I don't say this. I loved the way it felt when he wrapped me up in his wings at the castle, and part of me hopes that he'll do it again. I'm not ready to make love to him just yet, but I'm not averse to cuddling. "No. The bed is fine."

CHAPTER 13

SKYE

I tuck my hair behind my ear to hide the nervous pounding of my heart. Even though I love the idea of cuddling, I'm concerned about sharing a bed with Raidyn. I know he said we wouldn't mate until I'm ready, but I've never shared a bed with any man before, much less one I'm so attracted to.

So instead of heading inside, I sit in one of the balcony chairs. It's big enough for two people, so Raidyn takes a seat beside me. Warmth radiates from his body to mine and I shiver slightly, not because of the cool breeze but because of his nearness. His masculine scent—a strange mixture of cinnamon and spice—surrounds us. My heart hammers and I lift my gaze to the sky, staring up at the stars to calm my rapidly fraying nerves.

Maybe I wouldn't be so nervous if I didn't know what he wants. But when I turn toward him, I find his gaze locked on me and I feel lost. I'm in over my head. I curse myself again for reading all those romance novels on the ship because a thousand scenarios are playing out in my head, imagining how this night might end. Each ends with us panting heavily in each other's arms after making passionate love in the bed. Or the pool. Or on the balcony. Or in the gardens. Or even while flying above the tree line.

Oh my gosh. Did I really just imagine him flying us while we make love? I shake my head softly. I don't even know what his stav looks like or if we'll fit properly. Just thinking about it, a warm flush creeps from my neck to my cheeks and into my ears as heat pulses between my thighs.

"Are you all right?" he asks, concern evident in his features.

Unable to speak, I swallow thickly and nod.

His nostrils flare and his pupils dilate until only the barest rim of blue is visible around the edges. He can smell my arousal, and judging by the look on his face, my scent is affecting him.

I need to calm down. Drawing in a deep breath, I decide to distract him… and myself for that matter. Because the way he's looking at me now, so full of love and desire, I'm tempted to jump into his arms and allow him to ravish me, just like I've read in my romance novels. "So… tell me more about your world. How many Clans are there?"

"There are four: Wind, Fire, Water, and Earth."

"Have you always been divided?"

"No. Once, there were four brothers, each vying for their father's throne. A great war broke out and finally, they decided to split the territory and make peace. And thus, the four separate Clans came to be." His tone is practiced like he knows this history well.

"How long ago did this happen?"

"Thousands of cycles ago," he replies. "That was when

each Clan began developing different abilities. Some breathe fire, others firefrost. Only the Earth Clan also possess healing fire. They stayed neutral for millennia to share their Healing breath equally with all Clans." He lifts a thoughtful gaze to the sky. "I believe each Clan has at least one Earth Clan Healer living among them. They are honorable people."

"So... all the Clans trust them?" I ask, eager to understand as much as I can about this new world.

"Yes," he replies. "There have been periods of peace among all the Clans in our history. During those times, we held great gatherings, celebrations that were hosted in a different Clan's territory each cycle."

"When was the last celebration held?"

The ghost of a smile crests his lips as he lowers his gaze. "Shortly before the death of my mother, when I was still a child."

"And Varus, the prince of the Fire Clan—the one who has my friend—you said you were like brothers once."

He nods and I don't miss the sadness lying behind his eyes as he murmurs, "We were. Once. But in my anger over my mother's death, I pushed him away. Blamed him and his people for allowing her to die."

I take his hand and squeeze it gently. He lifts his pained gaze to me. "But you know they weren't responsible for her death, right? She loved you, Raidyn. It was her choice to save you."

He sighs heavily. "I realize that now, but I have been bitter for so long, and this," he points at his scar, "has only made it worse."

I frown in confusion. "Why?"

His expression shifts before he looks away as if hesitant to answer my question. I don't understand why.

I place my free hand on his forearm, drawing his attention back to me. "You don't have to tell me if you don't want to."

Sadness flits across his expression. "It is just... difficult," he finally admits. "The sandstorm that killed my mother also gave me this mark. I hit a rock and the wound was too deep for the Healers to completely repair. The scar is a painful reminder of her death and has become the reason that no female wants me."

I jerk my head back in shock. "Because of a scar?"

He nods. "It is a disfigurement. Drakarian females want only attractive, unblemished males."

I huff. "It's ridiculous to judge a man because of a scar."

He turns to me, studying me with intense curiosity. "It is not this way with your people?"

I shrug. "Some human women judge guys by their appearance, but not all."

"And you?"

I lift my gaze to find hope reflected in his eyes. "I just want a guy who cherishes and loves me as much as I do him."

Cautiously, he reaches out to cup my cheek, brushing the soft pad of his thumb across my skin. "I would give you all this and more," he whispers, "if you would be mine. My vow."

His gaze holds mine intently with a face so full of love and devotion, it steals the breath from my lungs. He leans in and gently presses his forehead to mine. Closing his eyes, he clenches his jaw.

"You already know how I feel." He places his hand over his chest, the scales glowing dimly beneath his palm. "And I will wait for as long as you need to decide if you want me as your mate."

Words lodge in my throat, but I somehow manage to voice them. "How do you know you truly love me? How do you know it's not just this *bond* that is making you feel that way?"

He sighs heavily, shaking his head. "You may as well ask me why the sun is bright or the moon only appears after it sinks beneath the horizon. These things just *are* and have always been, even in the time of my ancestors. Not all Drakarians are blessed with the fated bond, but those who are blessed do not question it. We embrace it for the beautiful gift that it is."

His response saddens me. I push away from him, staring down at my hands. "So my identity doesn't matter," I mumble despairingly. "This bond is all you need to know I'm the one for you."

He frowns. "You say this like it is a bad thing."

"Well, isn't it?" I ask incredulously. "You don't care who I am as long as you feel the bond."

He huffs, frustrated. "That is not the intention of the bond. It—"

A subtle noise downstairs draws Raidyn's attention. He freezes.

Panic spikes through my veins. "What is it?"

He stands, pulling me up and spreading his wings wide as if to shield me from danger. "Stay here," he mutters under his breath. "I must check downstairs."

I grip his forearm to stop him. "No. It might be dangerous. Stay with me."

He shakes his head. "Do you not know I would face down an entire legion of enemies to keep you safe?" He cups my cheek. "Please, my beautiful Skye. Wait here for me."

The sound of voices drifts up the stairs and I still beside him, gripping his forearm tighter. "Please, Raidyn. Don't go," I beg. "I don't want anything to happen to you."

"Is that you, Raidyn?" a voice calls up from below.

A smile crests his lips. "Yes, it is me. I am coming down."

I face him, frowning in confusion.

"They are the caretakers of the house."

"Friends of yours? You're sure they won't betray us?" I'm still hesitant to let him go.

"They would never betray me. Dyren and Mauryn are like family."

CHAPTER 14

SKYE

As we descend the stairs, I stay close to Raidyn's side. I'm not entirely sure I trust these people as much as he seems to. After all, what are they doing here in the middle of the night? Their timing is suspicious enough. But his posture seems completely relaxed as we make our way into the living room space.

A dragon man with light-gray scales and silver hair smiles brightly as soon as he sees Raidyn. The dark-gray, white-haired dragon woman beside him rushes forward to hug him. "It is so good to see you!"

"Likewise." Raidyn beams. "It has been too long."

When she pulls back, I step out from his back to stand by his side. She blinks several times, frozen. "Who is this?"

"I have never seen your species before," the man interjects almost simultaneously.

Raidyn wraps his arm around my waist and tugs me to his side. The scales on his chest glow brightly as he presents me to them. "Dyren, Mauryn. This is Skye. My linaya."

They gape at me. The woman—Mauryn—speaks first. "But... this is unprecedented. A fate bond outside of our species? How is this possible?"

"She is human," Raidyn explains. "Prince Varus of the Fire Clan has claimed another female of her kind as his linaya as well."

They look more astounded than ever.

"Skye," he turns to me, "this is Dyren and Mauryn. They are the caretakers of this home; they have known me since I was a child. They are like family to me."

Mauryn smiles warmly at him then rushes forward to embrace me as well. When she pulls back, she eyes me appraisingly, stifling a gasp. "You do not have any wings."

I shake my head. "My people don't fly."

"And no claws." Her gaze drifts to my hands. "Or scales or... fangs." Her eyes are full of worry as she faces Raidyn. "You must take great care with her. She has no natural defenses."

I would protest, but she's right. Drakarians are much taller and stronger than humans. Not to mention their dragon form.

Mauryn is the first female Drakarian I've seen up close, and she strikes me as formidable. She is as large in height and build as her husband. I'm nothing like the women of their species. Doubt begins to creep into my heart as I wonder why Raidyn would even want such a defenseless mate.

"She is stronger than she seems." He smiles and tilts his chin up with pride as he pulls me again to his side.

The sincerity in his words melts my heart and warmth fills my entire body. He really is proud to be attached to me. When he turns to me and flashes his devastatingly handsome smile, his gaze holds more love, pride, and devotion than I've ever received before.

Mauryn steps forward, still regarding Raidyn with

concern. "We heard there was trouble between you and your father." She shakes her head softly. "He just hasn't been the same male since your mother died."

Dyren adds, "We were worried about you, so we decided to come by and stock the stasis unit in case you came here. We anticipated that you might need a place to hide until your father comes to his senses."

Their words touch me. These people care for him deeply.

"Thank you," he says. "I appreciate it."

Mauryn gestures to some boxes behind them. "This is everything we brought to restock the stasis unit. If you should need anything else, simply contact us. It is safer for you to remain hidden here than to venture out for supplies."

As she says this, I think back on our night-time flight over the nearby city, hoping and praying that no one recognized him. Though when I glance at him, his relaxed shoulders tell me he isn't worried, and I trust him. If he's not concerned, then I won't be, either.

Mauryn looks aggrieved. "I do not think your father would look for you here, but you should be prepared if he does."

He nods. "I will set up a perimeter defense system."

"That should suffice," Dyren chimes in. "We will leave you two to your nest. If you need anything, please do not hesitate to let us know."

Our nest? My cheeks heat in embarrassment.

Mauryn approaches me, carefully placing one hand low on my abdomen. "May the Gods bless you with many fledglings."

I give her a nervous grin. Instead of arguing that we're not technically mates, I reply, "Thank you."

When they leave, I turn to Raidyn. Dyren's words replay in my mind—he called this house our nest. Images of Raidyn and I wrapped in each other's arms beneath the covers fill my mind.

He takes my hand. I swear, with the way he's looking at me, if he lifts me into his arms and takes me to the bed to ravish me like a romance novel hero, I won't protest. "I must set up a perimeter defense system. You should rest, my mate."

A strange mixture of disappointment and relief washes through me at his words. I don't have to make any decisions yet. Again, I don't argue when he calls me his mate. I tell myself it's because it's not worth an argument, but secretly, I'm beginning to like it when he calls me his. He declared it with so much pride to the caretaker and his wife, two people who are obviously very important to him.

He leaves and I head for the bedroom. I look around for pajamas but find none, so I guess I'll be sleeping in my robe. Raidyn's people probably sleep naked, since nudity doesn't seem to bother them in the slightest. However, I don't think I'm ready to go nude just yet.

I must be more tired than I realized because I fall asleep quickly. A dip in the mattress behind me rouses me. I recognize Raidyn the moment he slips beneath the comforter and his delicious scent fills my nostrils. He curls protectively around me, and I'm too exhausted to protest. I trust him. He won't try anything unless I consent.

Tonight, all I'm interested in is sleeping.

A soft puff of air parts the hair on top of my head as he scents me before gently nuzzling the spot and tugging me back into his chest. I rest my arm over the one he has draped around my waist.

"Good night," I whisper, closing my eyes as I allow myself to drift away.

CHAPTER 15

RAIDYN

I wake up curled protectively around my mate in the morning. My stav is fully extended from my mating pouch and painfully erect with the need to claim her. And though I'm sure we must be compatible to mate since we are fated, I do not know if she wants me, too.

Although she does not feel it yet, she is mine. I am already hers; I have been since the moment I first saw her. I would have loved her then, if she had accepted me, but now that I have spent more time with her, I find my love deepening.

My thoughts turn to my father and my cousin. How can they not see that it would be wrong to make the human females feel as if they had no choice but to pick a mate simply because they present them with eligible warriors? My father has truly gone mad beyond reason. I should have forced him to step down long ago.

But I did not want to see him brought low—not after losing my mother nearly broke him. In our grief, at least we were united. He allowed me to rule from the sidelines while he occupied the throne.

Tai warned me our arrangement might go wrong. His was a subtle warning, but still, I should not have ignored it. I didn't want to believe that my father was beyond rescue. And now my mate is in danger because of my carelessness—my inability to act promptly.

I could flee to the Fire Clan and seek asylum there. But what kind of life would that be for my Skye, to be bonded to an outsider?

Besides, despite his anger, my father loves me above all else. Would he truly let me go if I went to live among the Fire Clan?

I doubt it. He would blame my Skye—my linaya—for my leaving. And he would be right. He threatened to imprison her. I will not stay where she is threatened and I refuse to leave her side. Even if she does not want me as her mate, I desire only to care for her. I vow to do whatever I can to help her people make a life on our world.

As much as the thought pains me, my mate will never truly be safe until my father no longer sits on the throne.

She stirs softly, stretching her lithe body against mine. A small gasp escapes me when her backside rubs along my shaft; my stav throbs with need in response. Before I can restrain it, a low growl of arousal rumbles in my chest.

Skye stills for a moment, then slowly turns to face me, uncertainty written across her features.

I lower my gaze in shame. "Forgive me," I whisper. "I have never been this close to a female. It is…" I pause, casting about for the right word before settling on, "difficult."

Rational thought and even the ability to form words is difficult while she lies in my arms. Surrounded by her intoxicating scent, my entire body hums in awareness of her.

"It's all right." She smiles warmly. "I have never slept with a man. It's kind of awkward for me, too."

I am glad that she does not pull away from me as she might have done before. However, I do not want to push her into mating if she is not ready. So, reluctantly, I stand from the bed. As I do, my stav twitches, still fully erect and extended from my body.

Her eyes travel down my form and when she notices this, her lips part and her entire face flushes a deep crimson hue.

Curious about her reaction, I ask, "Do I resemble your human males?"

"Uh, I—um." She quickly averts her gaze as she stumbles over her words. "I think you're quite a bit larger and—uh—you have ridges." Her voice rises in pitch on the last word.

I frown. "Is that bad?"

She blinks up at me, her expression still a mask of astonishment, before she manages a nervous smile. "No. If anything, it's… good." She clears her throat. "At least, from what I've heard."

My nostrils flare as her delicate scent thickens and I realize that she is aroused by my appearance. I meet her deep-blue eyes evenly, my voice rough even to my own ears. "I can scent your need, my mate."

Her robe slips off her shoulder as she stares up at me, revealing the creamy, pale skin beneath. The delicate curve of her breast is just barely visible above the hem, but the memory of her soft, luscious body when I found her in the pool surfaces in my mind, sharpening my need. I desire more than anything to touch her, to feel her petal-soft skin beneath the tips of my fingers.

Her gaze travels down my form appraisingly again. Liquid beads on the tip of my stav and my every muscle tenses; I am desperate to claim her. Her small, pink tongue darts out to lick her lips. I cautiously move toward her.

She stands and we stare across the bed at one another. I want nothing more than to pull her into my arms and bury myself in her warmth, but I will not push her to do anything she does not want. I will wait for her to decide what we will do.

She steps closer and gently reaches out to skim the tips of her fingers across my chest. My scales light, glowing with the fate bond beneath her touch as she stares at them in fascination and wonder.

"They seem brighter now," she whispers. "Why?"

"Because you are so near," I rasp, my entire form tense with desire.

She trails her hands down to my abdomen, tracing the dips and curves of my muscles as if memorizing me by touch. "You're beautiful," she whispers.

I catch her eyes with mine. "You are perfect, Skye."

"Perfect?" She smiles.

I reach out and tuck a stray tendril of her long, golden hair behind her ear then gently cup her cheek. "Yes, you are. Give yourself to me, my beautiful mate. Allow me to worship you."

She lowers her gaze. "I... I don't know. I just..." She lifts her head and her blue eyes search mine. "How do you know you want *me* and it's not just the bond influencing you?"

Her questions are strange, and I do not understand her hesitation. "This is the way of things, Skye. The Gods have fated us to be together."

Something about my answer displeases her and she steps back. "Can you please put on some clothes?"

I regard her curiously. "Why?"

"Because it's... distracting that you're naked."

I heave a sigh of frustration and will my stav to retract into my mating pouch. I wish I could do as she asks, even if I do not understand why. "I cannot wear clothing, as I had planned on shifting forms. My draka form is much larger than this one, so my clothing would not survive the transformation intact."

She nods. "Oh, right. I hadn't thought of that."

I tip my head to the side. "Why are you so averse to my nudity?"

"My people only get naked when…" Her voice trails off.

"When what?" I ask, genuinely curious.

Her eyes snap up to meet mine and her cheeks turn dark red yet again. "When we're going to mate."

"Ah. Now I understand." I arch a teasing brow. "So, when you are ready to mate, will you bare yourself to me as the signal of your acceptance?"

She hesitates a moment before answering. "When I'm ready, I'll let you know."

I note that she did not tell me, as she has before, that she might never wish to mate with me. Instead, she told me that she will let me know *when* she is ready to mate. This is progress, at least. She is starting to consider becoming mine.

My stav presses insistently against the inside seam of my mating pouch and I struggle to calm down. She does not want me—yet. But I am a patient male. I will prove to her that I will be a good mate. And when she is convinced, she will open her heart, her mind, and her body to me, allowing me to fully claim her.

"Why are you shifting forms again?" she asks, pulling me from my errant thoughts.

"To check our perimeter defense."

"Oh. Can I come with you?"

Normally, I would deny her, but I doubt anyone is searching for me here, so there is very little danger of discovery. And even so, she is safer with me than in the house by herself.

While together, if we are discovered, I'd at least have the

chance to escape with her again. Whereas if she was found here without me and taken, I would have difficulty rescuing her from my father's guards.

Unless they are still loyal to me. There is only a handful whom I know would still obey my command. The rest... I am uncertain.

"Yes, you may accompany me," I tell her. An idea occurs to me. "But first, let us pack some food for our trip."

"Trip?" she asks. "How far are we going?"

"Not far. But there is a waterfall on this island that I think you might enjoy."

I am rewarded with one of her brilliant smiles. "All right."

We pack a light meal and then she climbs onto my back. I am glad I chose to travel in my draka form during this day since I am stronger and more capable of defending her against enemies.

She releases a joyful cry as I spread my wings and we take to the air.

I also prefer this form because it allows me to sense her thoughts. She loves flying with me.

As I dip to the left to catch another current, the muscles of my back flex beneath her legs. She clenches her thighs to hold tighter to me and her thoughts turn without warning towards desire. Images of my nude form, my stav fully extended and erect, fill her mind.

My mouth drifts open as she imagines touching me and allowing me to touch her in return. My heart hammers as she visualizes me grabbing her waist and hauling her against my form. She wraps her arms around my neck and her legs around my waist as I thrust my hips repeatedly against hers, driving my stav deep into her channel.

The scent of her need fills my nostrils and a low growl of arousal rumbles in my chest. She wants me. She imagines us mating in several different ways. On the bed, in the bath, in the gardens, on the balcony, in a pool beneath the waterfall.

I hold onto that image in my mind, beating my powerful wings to circle the perimeter and check that no trespassers have crossed the invisible barrier I've set up in defense. I cannot wait to reach the falls and find out if she will ask me to mate with her there.

Surely that is why such erotic thoughts of me claiming her fill her mind.

I will oblige her gladly.

Satisfied that our perimeter defense is still intact, I fly as fast as my wings can carry me to the waterfall on the island. It is near the house, but far enough to afford us privacy if Dyren and Mauryn return for an unexpected visit.

If my mate wants me to claim her, I do not want to be interrupted.

As I touch down on the ground, I shift instantly so that I can gently lower her down my body with my hands around her slim waist.

She smiles up at me and I take her hand to lead her to the expansive pool at the base of the falls. Crystal-clear, sparkling water tumbles over the rocky ledge above, spilling into the basin below. I ask her if she'd like to get in after we eat, remembering how she fantasized that I'd take her in the water beneath the falls.

If she agrees to our first mating, I want to make sure she is well-fed before we begin. I plan on taking her several times once she decides to be mine and allows me to fully claim her.

"That sounds good." She smiles again.

My heart hammers in my chest as I unpack our small

satchel of food and sit beside her. She is so close, the warmth of her body radiates against mine as we eat our meal.

"It's so beautiful here," she comments. "You are so lucky to have grown up in paradise."

I turn to her. "There are many beautiful places on Drakaria, and I would like to show you many more if you will let me."

"I would like that," she murmurs as she lies back in the thick blanket of grass.

Her long, silken hair spreads out beneath her like a beautiful golden halo and my fingers ache with the urge to comb through the soft strands.

Feeling bold, I lie beside her and gently place my hand atop hers. She surprises me by turning her palm up toward mine and entwining our fingers. "It's nice spending time with you."

I grin. "I am glad that you are happy."

Her expression falls, sadness pooling in her deep blue eyes.

"What is wrong, my Skye?"

"I'm sorry for all the trouble I've caused you. If not for me, you wouldn't have to hide."

I roll onto my side to face her, gently stroking her cheek. "Do you not know that I would give up my entire world just to keep you safe?"

Tears gather in the corner of her eyes, but she says nothing.

"I love you, Skye. You are a blessing I never imagined could be mine. I would do anything to keep you from harm and to see you happy, my beautiful mate."

A tear slips down her cheek, which she quickly brushes away.

"Do not cry, my mate. I am here and I will take care of you. I will protect you from all danger. My vow."

She smiles, softly biting her lower lip before she reaches out and traces her delicate fingers along the sharp ridge of my brow. She studies me intently as if memorizing the contours of my face. I lean into her touch and close my eyes as a deep growl of pleasure vibrates my chest.

She laughs, pink blooming across her cheeks.

My eyes snap open. "What is so funny?"

With a soft sigh, she does her best to suppress a smile as she shakes her head. "You really need to wear some clothes when we're alone."

"If that is what you wish, I will need you to carry them for me so that I can put them on after I shift." I blink several times, unnerved. "Does my nudity bother you so much?"

I anxiously await her answer. I thought she desired me, but if she keeps insisting I wear clothing, my form must offend her in some way.

"No, it doesn't bother me. Quite the opposite." She grins. "I'd rather carry something to put over your mouth to stop you from saying things that distract me even more."

I tip my head to the side. "I do not understand."

She reaches out to cup my cheek and I note sadness lingers behind her eyes, as it did the other night when she asked me if I would still want her without the bond. "I'm... falling in love with you, Raidyn. But, I—" Her voice catches and she lowers her gaze.

I place two fingers under her chin and tip her face back up. "What is it? Why is it so wrong to allow yourself to be mine? I am already yours, my linaya."

A tear slips down her cheek. "That's the problem. You only want me because of the bond. Without it, I don't know if you would even see me."

My brow furrows deeply. "We cannot change what is, my Skye. The bond exists between us. Of this, I have no doubt." I take her hand and place it on my chest, directly over my glowing scales. "Many question the fate bond because they are uncertain about the partner the Gods have chosen for them. I did not—and have never—felt this hesitation toward you.

"You are a strong female. Fire burned in your eyes when you fought the male who attacked you. And when you thought I meant you harm, you fought me as well. Even after being thrown in a cell, you stood up to my father—the King. I admire your strength of spirit." I stroke her cheek and stare deep into her eyes with a smile. "Despite your lack of natural defenses, you have a strong will that rivals any Drakarian female's. I was proud when you threatened my guard, Tai; despite your fear, there is admirable fire in your heart. I am proud that the Gods have paired us. I am proud to be yours and I want so desperately for you to be mine as well."

She watches me silently and I wonder if I have said too much.

"Forgive me," I tell her. "I do not wish to make you uncomfortable."

She cuts me off by leaning forward and gently pressing her lips to mine.

I'm so shocked, I do not move or dare to breathe as I wait to see what she will do next. This touching of lips is not customary among my people and I am uncertain how to respond. I saw this in her mind, but... I do not know what it means.

She pulls back and looks up at me, a small frown creasing her brow. "Do your people not kiss?"

"*Kiss?*" I ask, touching my lips. "Is that what this is?"

She nods.

"Is it part of your mating ritual?"

She flushes a deep red. "Sort of. But do you mind if this is all we do?"

My brows shoot up to my forehead. *Do I mind?* I would

give anything to feel her mouth on mine again. "I do not mind at all. I am just unsure of what to do."

"Luckily for you," she smiles, "I, at least, have some experience with this."

A growl threatens to rise in my throat at the thought of another male touching her in this way, but I force it back down. That was before she met me. Now that I am here, I will endeavor to kiss her so often and so well, she will never think of any male who came before me.

She cups my face, leaning closer to touch her mouth lightly to mine. Her lips are soft and warm. I gasp as she runs her tongue along my lower lip as if asking for entrance. I open my mouth and when her tongue finds mine, I am lost.

It is soft and smooth like the rest of her form, whereas my tongue is ridged. She moves her tongue along mine and I groan low in my throat at the delicious sensation. How have my people never discovered this custom?

Her taste is exquisite and as her tongue curls around mine, I want more. I want to possess her as she has possessed me—mind, body, and soul. I cup the back of her neck and hold her in place as I deepen our kiss, plunging my tongue into her mouth as I long to sheathe my stav deep in her channel.

A soft moan escapes her and I pull her even closer. She climbs into my lap while my stav extends, seeking the warmth of her center. The scent of her arousal thickens the air. Only the thin barrier of her robe separates us, her wet heat soaking through the fabric as she moves her hips insistently against mine.

I release a tortured groan. It would be so easy to pull back her robe and bare her to my eyes. I ache to bury myself inside her. To fill her with my seed and claim her as mine. My nostrils flare as the scent of her need strengthens.

Though she claimed her people do not go into heat, when

she grips my shoulders, digs her nails into my back, and rolls her hips against mine, it is obvious she desires me as much as I do her.

I love the feel of her petal-soft skin beneath the tips of my fingers as I trace them down her form. When I reach the curve of her breast, I am surprised by how easily the soft flesh gives beneath my touch. Drakarian females do not have any softness here.

I brush my thumb across the peak and she gasps, her kisses becoming more desperate as her nipple becomes a hard beaded tip beneath my palm. When I roll the stiff peak between my thumb and forefinger, she gasps and arches into my palm as if begging for more.

"This is," I gasp between kisses, "sensitive?"

"Yes," she breathes into my mouth. "I want your hands all over me."

Encouraged by her response, I cup her other breast to give it the same attention.

She takes my hand and moves it down her body. My heart hammers as she guides me to her center. "Touch me here," she whispers with a half-lidded gaze.

I dip my fingers between her soft folds, pleased to find that she is already slick with arousal. She guides me to a small pearl of flesh at the apex and as soon as my finger brushes against it, she moans and her entire body seems to light up with pleasure.

"Right there," she mumbles against my lips.

I continue to tease at the sensitive flesh as she writhes in my lap. I groan as the hard length of my stav drags through her warm, wet heat.

I explore her body, and as soon as I find the entrance to her channel, she arches into my hand. Carefully, I press the tip of my finger into her tight heat and she gasps.

Heavy-lidded eyes meet mine. "Raidyn," she pleads. "More."

My entire body is tense with need. I'm desperate to claim her, but she is not ready for a full mating yet. However, she desires my touch, and I will take anything she is willing to give me. And even if we never fully mate, holding her in my arms, her body pressed against mine, is enough. I hug her tightly and drop my head into the space between her neck and shoulders, inhaling deeply of her intoxicating scent as she kneads the muscles along my back and grinds herself against me.

"I long to taste you on my tongue," I whisper against her skin.

She stills and I worry that I have said too much; that I have asked for more than I should. But she pulls away to lie on her back. I watch as she undoes the fastening of her robe and it falls away, revealing her bare form to my gaze. She is perfect; I have never seen a more beautiful sight in my entire life.

She reaches for me and I surge toward her. Curling her hand around the back of my neck, she pulls my lips back down to hers. I worry my weight could crush her beneath me, so I brace my elbows on either side of her body as she deepens our kiss.

The tip of my stav bumps against her entrance and she inhales sharply. Her tongue curls around mine and I long more than anything to join our bodies as one. But when I pull back just enough to search her gaze, hesitation is evident in her eyes. I will not fully claim her until she is ready, but I want to give her pleasure. "Please, allow me to taste you, my beautiful mate."

She nods and I move down her body, trailing a line of soft kisses down her petal-soft skin. I run my hands along her inner thighs to part them, baring her fully to my gaze. The hesitation spreads across her features, and she starts to close her thighs. I remove my hands and gaze up at her. "We will do nothing you do not wish."

She sits up, pulling her robe to cover her body, then nestles against me.

"I'm sorry," she whispers. "It's just... I've never done this before and I—"

I press a kiss to her forehead and cup her jaw, tipping her head back to look up at me. "It is fine, my mate. We can wait."

I hold her tightly to me. She is perfect, my Skye. I will wait as long as she needs me to. This night, she has allowed me to touch her more intimately than I could have ever dreamt.

CHAPTER 16

SKYE

As I nestle against him, I notice his scales glowing much brighter than they ever have before. I trace my fingers over the swirling pattern, curious. "They've brightened. Why is that?"

"Because you are so close to me," he replies. "When fated mates complete their bonding, joining their bodies as one, the pattern will remain steadfast and glowing so all may know they are a fully mated pair."

I think about his father, remembering the same pattern on his scales. "I saw something similar on your father's chest, but the glow had gone dark."

He nods. "Because my mother is dead, it will never glow again."

Only now do I realize that I did not see this pattern on any other Drakarians. "Does everyone wait to find their linaya? Or do some mate simply because they fall in love?"

"Not all find their fated mate. And now that there are so few females, the bond is even rarer."

I remember he told me about the Great Plague that killed many Drakarian women and rendered the rest infertile. My mind drifts back to the flu that burned through our ships three years ago, the dark memories returning like a tide to the shore.

"I'm sorry your people have suffered so much loss," I tell him. "We lost many as well during the viral outbreak that took my parents a few years ago. A strain of the flu swept through on our colony ships. We lost almost half our people during that time."

"My hearts grieve with yours," he whispers into my hair.

"Thank you."

"Before the Great Plague, nearly as many females as males lived on Drakaria; most waited until they found their fated one before forming a pair bond. Now, we are so desperate we have begun negotiations with other Clans to discuss the possibility of intermating." He looks down. "Some of our Healers predict that due to the lack of females, we may be facing the extinction of our race."

"What about mating with other species?"

"We have been a spacefaring race for hundreds of cycles, but ever since the plague, we keep mostly to ourselves. Our Healers believe that one of our trading ships brought the virus that devastated our population. After the plague, we did search for other species who may be biologically compatible but found none. So, we gave up on searching."

Listening to the history of his people, I realize how desperate they are for females, which concerns me. I fix him with a serious look. "What if our two species are not capable of having children?"

He cups my cheeks, his deep-blue eyes staring into mine. "It would not matter to me. I would still desire you. The Gods have gifted you to me and I will not ignore or turn away such a perfect blessing."

His words fill me with warmth, and I smile.

He returns a tender look. "After my mother died following the Great Plague, I was angry at the Gods. I blamed them for my people's every misfortune. I turned my back on their teachings." He shakes his head softly. "I was shunned by many females because of my disfigurement, which only added to my resentment. But the moment I found you, I rediscovered my faith. The Gods had not deserted me after all—they gave me a fated one. A gift that not everyone receives."

I swallow against the lump in my throat as doubt begins to creep in once again. I slowly untangle myself from his arms and sit back. "So it *is* the bond that makes you love me."

"No," he denies vehemently. "It is *you* that makes me love you. I want you and only you, Skye. For the first time, I am grateful to the Gods for giving me my scar. In giving me this scar, they made sure that the right female would find me. One that could look beyond it and see me for who I am instead of my title. If I had not had this scar, I would likely already have been mated. And if I had been mated to another and then discovered you after, it would have been the most devastating tragedy of my existence."

He reaches out to cup my cheek. "When I look at you, I feel as if I have found the other half of my soul. I have told you more in the past few days than I have told even those closest to me. I can open my heart and bare my thoughts to you in a way that I never could with others." His brow furrows softly. "Do you not feel the same?"

His words touch me deeply because this is exactly how I feel. I take his hand, lifting it to my chest as I entwine our fingers. "Although I still don't understand it, I know that this," I gesture to our joined hands, "feels right like nothing else ever has."

He flashes his devastatingly handsome smile and I can

feel my tower of logic crumbling all around me as my heart insists that I allow myself to fall for him.

I continue. "But it scares me a bit, too, Raidyn. I... I'm new to all of this. I've only ever read about love in books. I never thought it would ever happen for me in real life."

He pulls me back into his arms and wraps his wings around my form. He lifts my hand to his chest, resting my open palm over the luminescent pattern on his scales. "This is proof that such love exists, but I can understand your hesitation because it is not natural for your people. There is no rush, my Skye. We can take as much time as you want. We have the rest of our lives to get to know one another, and I will wait for however long you need to decide whether you want me or not."

A tear slips down my cheek. How many dates have I gone on, hoping and praying to meet a man like Raidyn, only to find out they were only interested in one thing? I never thought I'd be so lucky, and I've never felt more loved as I do in this moment.

But even as happiness blooms in my heart, I feel incredibly selfish. Here I am, making out with Raidyn, while I have no idea how Lilliana is doing. Is she happy? Is she safe? What about the rest of our crew?

Raidyn gently nuzzles my temple. "What is wrong?"

"I was just thinking about my friends. Especially Lilliana," I tell him. "I know you said Varus would never hurt her, but I need to see for myself that she's all right. She has always been like a sister to me, and now that the rest of my family is gone, she is all I have left."

CHAPTER 17

RAIDYN

As we fly back to the house, myriad thoughts flit through her mind. Her tangled emotions are so complex, I am unable to discern what they mean. She cares for me, but she is conflicted. And she worries about her friend and the rest of her people.

I am worried about them, too. The Fire Clan has no doubt discovered them by now, but I must be certain. We will have to search the desert near the site where I found Skye. Even if we do find them, I cannot take them back to the Wind Clan. I would have no choice but to take them to Prince Varus. He is not dishonorable like my cousin who whispers poison in my father's ear.

When I set Skye down on the balcony, she lingers by my side. "What are you thinking about?"

"My father," I reluctantly admit. "He and my cousin are wrong to think that they could present your people with eligible males and tell them they must choose a mate from among them. I know your species could be the answer to our problems, but it would be wrong in so many different ways to force them into making a choice they may not be ready to make."

She studies me curiously. "What do you mean?"

I place my hand on my chest. "I know you are concerned we may be unable to have fledglings, but I do not believe the Gods would have fated us if we were not biologically compatible. What if some of the other unmated human females are destined to others of my kind?" I shake my head softly in frustration. "And my father and cousin would insist they take only members of the Wind Clan as their mates, keeping them all for themselves, denying the males in other Clans the opportunity to find their linaya. What a horrible thing it would be if a Drakarian mates with another's linaya and later discovers the mistake."

"Has that happened before?"

"Never. At least, it has never been recorded." I look to the stars. "Who knows what happens in the other Clans? We have been separated for so long. We hardly share information with one another anymore."

"Don't you think that weakens you as a people?"

I study her, curious to hear her outsider perspective. "How so?"

"If the Clans are so separated, it only creates a further divide between your race." She tilts her head to the side, something I notice she does when she is in deep thought. "How can your species remain strong? If something drastic, like another disease outbreak or an invasion, were to happen, how would you coordinate an effort to fight it? Don't you see how much trouble your division could cause?"

She speaks truth. The Clans have been acting like our ancestors, the four brothers—treating our brethren like enemies.

We are the same species, blessed by the same Gods,

despite the slight differences in our appearance and abilities. Instead of widening the gap between Clans with fighting and mistrust, we need to overcome our differences and unify our species.

Perhaps the humans were sent to us not only to be our linayas—our gifts from the Gods—but to teach us how to unite once more.

"You are right," I sigh. "Though I don't know how to even begin improving relations with the other Clans."

She sends me a look I cannot quite discern, but her faint smile doesn't reach her eyes. It seems my words have upset her. Probably because she is thinking of her friend and wondering if she will ever see her again now that she knows our Clans are so divided. "Someone has to be the first to try," she says. A yawn escapes her before she can cover her mouth. Her cheeks darken in response. "I think it's time for me to go to bed."

"I will join you."

She looks over her shoulder. "I think I'll sleep on the couch tonight."

My brows draw down. "You wish to sleep alone?"

She nods.

Part of me hopes she merely wants to take things slowly, but another part knows that something is wrong. Has she already made her decision? Is she rejecting me after all?

Even if she does not want me, I am not a male who would ever put his comfort above a female's. "You take the bed," I tell her. "I will sleep on the couch."

"You don't have to—" she starts to protest but I raise my hand in a bid to allow me to speak.

"No. I insist," I state firmly. "I will sleep on the sofa."

She nods and heads for the cleansing room. "I'm going to bathe first."

As soon as the door to the cleansing room closes, a

terrible thought fills my mind. I have not bathed since we arrived, since my scales naturally repel water and dirt. Drakarians do not bathe but every three or four days. She, however, has bathed twice now in two days, so human skin must need more frequent washing.

What if she finds my odor offensive? Her sense of smell must be very acute.

I must remedy this at once.

When she is finished, I make use of the cleansing pool as well. I take great care to scrub and thoroughly buff my scales to a pearlescent sheen.

Why did I not think to do this earlier?

What male does not groom to impress a female? I have been a fool, simply assuming she'd run into my arms because of the bond when all this time she has insisted that she does not sense its pull as I do. I have been expecting her to accept me without making any attempt to court her and entice her to become my mate.

As soon as I return to the bedroom, I find her already asleep. I'm disappointed since I wanted to see her reaction not only to the soap I used but to the polished finish of my freshly buffed scales. I checked my appearance several times in the mirror and am certain she will find my efforts pleasing. But that will have to wait until tomorrow, for I refuse to wake her now. It has been a long day for my mate; I will leave her to rest.

With a heavy sigh, I curl up on the couch and close my eyes, attempting to drift off to sleep.

My arms ache with the urge to hold her as I did last night, but she does not want this, and I will not push for anything she does not want.

My thoughts turn to the waterfall, where she responded so beautifully to my touch. My mind replays the small sounds of pleasure that escaped her as her tongue curled around mine and I explored her body. I am honored that she allowed me to worship her so intimately.

My stav extends from my mating pouch as I dwell on the memory. My entire body aches with the longing to hold her close again. Her entire form is soft and giving, unlike the females of my species, who are just as heavily muscled as the males.

A small whimper pierces the darkness and my eyes snap open to find her thrashing on the bed beneath the covers. I rush to her side and gently place a hand on her shoulder. Her eyes are still closed in sleep and I realize she must be having a nightmare.

"Skye, wake up. You are dreaming." I speak in a hushed tone to avoid startling her.

Her eyelids flutter open, her gaze searching the darkness for a moment before focusing on me. "Raidyn?" Her voice quavers softly.

I take her hand in mine and give it a reassuring squeeze. "I am here."

A broken sob escapes her as tears slip down her cheeks. "I couldn't save him, Raidyn," she whispers. "I couldn't save him."

"Save whom?"

"My brother, Thomas. I was supposed to protect him." She turns, pulling her knees up to her chest as she curls into a ball. "I left him behind. How could I do that?"

Her shoulders shake with sobs. The saline scent of her tears fills my nostrils. Despite her refusal to share a bed with me, I cannot help but gather her smaller form to my chest. I want only to comfort her.

The image of the young male in her arms, his eyes open but unseeing, flits through my mind. I realize now that this must be the memory she carries of his death.

"I wish I could take this pain from you," I run my hand

soothingly up and down her back. "I am sorry you lost your brother."

"He was the last of my family." Her voice breaks on the last word. "I was supposed to take care of him, Raidyn. I promised my mother on her deathbed that I would protect him, and I failed. We were so close to the escape pods and then suddenly," she draws in a shaking breath, "he was gone."

"*Shhh*," I whisper against her ear. "It is not your fault that your ship was attacked."

"But how could I just leave him?"

"If you had stayed, you would have died as well, my linaya. I do not think he would have wanted that." I pull back just enough to cup her face with both hands, gently brushing her tears away with my thumbs as I meet her eyes evenly. "It is not your fault that your brother died, my beloved."

Reluctantly, she nods, and I pull her back to my chest as she cries.

I suddenly realize we carry the same pain, she and I—the guilt of having survived when our loved ones did not. We both believe beyond reason that we could have done something differently to save them.

How many times have I lamented the fact that I survived because of my mother's sacrifice? If I could, I would have taken her place without hesitation. But I realize that if she had lived instead of me, my mother would have carried the same pain that I bear now.

My mate has lost so much in her life. First, her parents, and now, her brother. I gently run my hands through her long, silken hair as she slowly drifts off into a fitful sleep. I whisper in her ear, "Do not worry, my mate. I will make sure you see your friend again. We will travel to the Fire Clan territory and find her for you. My vow."

As she lies sleeping in my arms, I am hesitant to leave her side. However, I must respect her wish to sleep alone. I move to untangle our limbs so I can return to the couch, but her small hand on my forearm stops me abruptly.

"Wait," she mumbles, her blue eyes squinting up at me. "Stay here with me."

I nod, but as I move to lie down beside her, she makes a small sound of protest in the back of her throat and I still. "What is wrong?"

She looks hesitant. "Can you put on some clothes? A robe, at least?"

I have been nude almost the entire time we have been together. She has already seen my stav, but her insistence that I cover myself makes me worry again that she finds my form displeasing, despite how she reacted to my touch earlier.

"Yes." I hesitate for a moment, not wanting to ask, but I am desperate to know. She knows I will not mate her unless she wishes it. "Does my appearance offend you?"

My heart hammers as I wait anxiously for her reply. I should be accustomed to females finding me lacking by now. After all, how many have rejected me because of my scar? But if my fated one finds me unpleasant to regard, I believe the devastation will crush me.

Her cheeks turn a deep shade of red. "Clothing would offer a barrier," she hedges.

I stare at her in confusion. "Against what?"

She softly bites her lower lip as she averts her gaze. "Anything happening between us."

Her answer dismays me. I swallow against the bile rising in my throat, devastated that she suspects I might force myself upon her. "Do you really believe I would try to mate with you without your consent? I would sooner end my life than hurt you in any way, my beautiful linaya."

She reaches up to stroke my cheek with a shy smile. "It's not that. It's just... distracting. That's all. I'm worried I might be tempted to do something I'm not entirely ready for."

Despair turns to relief at her words. My chest swells with pride as soon as I realize what she has implied: She finds my appearance *too* pleasing. Happiness brighter than a thousand stars fills me as I leave quickly to retrieve a robe. A robe can be easily removed in case *she* becomes tempted to mate with me. I will not pass up the opportunity if she changes her mind and decides to claim me tonight.

After I change into a long gray robe, I lie down beside her. I want to wrap my arms around her, but I resist. If she wants my touch, she must be the one to initiate. After a moment, she rolls toward me and rests her head on my shoulder and her hand on my chest, directly between my two hearts. The glowing fate bond pattern flares to life at her touch as warmth suffuses my body. I tug her close to my side, pleased when she nestles into my touch.

I lie awake, listening to the sound of her breaths softening as she drifts off. She trembles and I realize she must be cold, so I tug the blanket up around her shoulders to warm her.

I must take great care to serve her needs. She is fragile, my mate. With no wings, fangs, claws, or scales, I wonder how her people have managed to survive as a species.

My father was shocked that they possess weapons powerful enough to pierce our scales. How can he not realize that such a race would need to develop weapons for defense? They are not dangerous; they are simply trying to survive. Would we not have done the same in their place?

It is still dark when she gently stirs in my arms. She lifts her head with a momentary, sleepy smile before her expression falters.

"What is wrong?"

She hesitates. "When you called my people the answer to your problems... it bothered me."

My brows knit together in confusion. "How so?"

"You said Lilliana is like me—fated to a Drakarian."

I nod, waiting patiently for her to continue.

"What will happen to us when word gets out that this is possible? I mean, you told me the bond had never happened outside of your species before and... you don't have many women left."

My mouth drifts open as understanding dawns upon me. She is worried my people will force human females to mate with Drakarian males. I move quickly to reassure her. "No Drakarian of any Clan would ever force-mate a female."

"But you were upset that the Fire Clan might find my crew before the Wind Clan did."

"Yes," I admit. I do not know how to explain myself to her, but I must try. I take her hand in mine and meet her gaze evenly. "If the Fire Clan had found you before I did, they would have taken you to their capital city, and I might never have met you. I might never have known you were my fated one. I only wish for others to have the same chance. What if more human females are fated by the Gods to be joined with a warrior from another Clan?"

"But what if they don't want to be?"

"Please, believe me when I tell you that no female will come to harm, just as I would never harm you. My vow."

"You say that," she counters, "but your father's actions tell me otherwise. Do you understand?"

With a clenched jaw, I lower my gaze. She is right to worry. I hate that my father has caused her to fear, to doubt that her people will be safe on Drakaria.

"My father is mad," I explain. "He has not been completely sane since my mother died. After we find your friends and your crew, I will go back to him and make him see reason." I meet her eyes evenly. "I will make certain he cannot threaten you or your people, my Skye. I will protect you. My vow."

She snuggles closer to me and I grit my teeth as my stav extends from my mating pouch, stirred by her proximity and the brush of her leg against mine.

She must feel my reaction, because she inhales sharply. The scent of her need fills the air. I dip my head to the curve of her neck and shoulder, and draw her delicious scent deep into my lungs.

CHAPTER 18

SKYE

My entire body flushes with warmth as he scents along my neck. His stav is hard against my body and I've never been so aroused in my entire life. The last thing I need is more temptation. Especially as I recall all those thick cords of muscle and the hard planes of his abdomen and chest. Warmth blooms in my core as I think of our make-out session by the falls.

He pulls back and a low growl rumbles deep in his chest as he rasps. "Forgive me, my mate. Your scent…it calls to me."

I shiver slightly as desire ripples through me. I nestle into his warmth. "It's all right. I trust you," I whisper.

However, wrapped in his arms, I'm not entirely sure that I trust myself. Every part of me wants him. I'm falling hard for this man and the reasons I've held back are beginning to crumble under his ice-blue gaze.

He doesn't speak, but he doesn't have to. Carefully, he wraps his wings around me and I sigh in contentment at the sensation of his warmth enveloping me completely. I try to fall back asleep, but it's impossible while his arousal is a hard bar between us, pressing insistently against my abdomen.

I open my eyes to find him staring down at me, his expression full of love and devotion. "Do you always watch the people you sleep with?" I grin.

He looks taken aback by my question. "I have never slept with anyone before."

"No other females?" I ask, shocked. He is a Prince, after all. Even if women rejected him as a mate because of his scar, I figured there would still be some who were willing to sleep with him simply because of his title and status.

He shakes his head. "My people mate for life. We do not sleep together casually like some species do." He pauses. "Is it the same with yours?"

"Well, some people wait to have sex until after they get married. I mean, *bonded*," I correct, making sure to use words he'll understand. "But others mate while they're dating, which doesn't necessarily mean they commit to staying together forever, you know. It's different for every human. Some people don't want to be tied down to a mate, so they never bond."

When I look up, his eyes are full of concern. "And what about you?"

Heat blooms across my cheeks and the bridge of my nose as I look away. My voice is barely a whisper as I shyly admit, "I've never had sex. I've never even shared a bed with anyone before you. Well, I have technically shared a bed with my female friends. But just for companionship, not for... mating." He blinks and I continue, stumbling over my words. "Not that there would be anything wrong with that, I'm just into men. Not women."

He studies me curiously. "Is it normal for human females to seek companionship with one another through touch?"

"I suppose so." His question strikes me as odd. "Why?"

"Because our females are very territorial. They do not normally associate with one another because they view other females as potential rivals."

"What about Drakarian men?" I ask. "Are they territorial?"

"Only recently, due to the lack of females. Once we find our mate, it is instinct to protect her. The desire to nest and provide for our mate and fledglings makes us very territorial against other males." He cocks his head to the side. "Are humans not this way?"

I shrug. "We can be. To be honest, I think things would be a lot simpler for humans if we had fated mates like you, and marks to tell everyone who's taken and who isn't."

A smirk twists his lips. "Then you are fortunate that I bear the mark for us both. I will display our bond to every one of your people so that they know that you are mine."

His words make me smile even as lingering doubt threatens to steal my joy. I haven't agreed to be his mate yet. Though my heart has already decided, my brain keeps insisting that I hold back and tread carefully.

His people do not have casual sex. So, as much as I'm attracted to him, nothing can happen between us until I'm completely sure.

CHAPTER 19

SKYE

Sunlight spills in through the open window, casting a soft glow throughout the bedroom. I snuggle into Raidyn's warm embrace, enjoying the feel of his larger form wrapped around mine.

It has only been a week since we escaped the castle and came to the cabin, but it feels like so much longer. Raidyn is so caring and gentle. Despite his fierce and intimidating appearance, he's so tender with me.

He takes me to the falls every day for a picnic and we spend a lot of time walking in the gardens around the cabin. It always ends with us making out, but we never do anything more than kissing and holding each other close.

I want him, but I'm also trying to take things slow. I've never been one to just jump into something so quickly. And I think that's part of what scares me. I never thought it was possible to fall so hard and so fast.

He asks questions about my life on the ship and about my family. It's been so long since I've talked about them and it feels good to be able to grieve over Thomas with someone who not only cares, but listens.

Still lying in bed, I prop myself up on one elbow as I look to him. "My brother would have liked you, you know."

He smiles. "From what you have shared, I believe I would have liked him as well."

"He always loved dragons, myths, and fairy tales. All the things that you, your people and this place remind me of. This world is…it's almost magical, Raidyn. Your species is blessed to call this planet home."

"It is your home now too, my Skye." He takes my hand in his. "I wish my mother had lived to meet you. She would have been thrilled that I found such a perfect mate."

I look down at myself and then arch a brow at him. "You don't think she would have been upset that I don't have claws, wings or fangs?"

Pulling me back into his arms, he hugs me close to his chest. He gives me a handsome smile as he tucks a stray tendril of hair behind my ear, staring at me as if I were a rare and precious treasure. "Even without all those things you are perfect, my beautiful mate."

His words melt my heart and I nestle even closer to him. He makes me feel so safe and warm and loved.

He curls his tail around my thigh as if anchoring me to him. He dips his nose to the curve of my neck and inhales deeply.

"Your scent," he growls.

Worried, I ask, "Do I smell bad?"

"No." His voice is a low rumble. "Your scent is intoxicating."

I'm suddenly aware of his hardened length pressing against my abdomen. Heat pulses in my core at the memory of his touch. I wonder what his stav would feel like deep inside me.

He inhales sharply, dragging me closer. I still when his stav pushes between my thighs. He quickly releases me and pulls away.

"Forgive me," he whispers. "The scent of your need is so strong, I—"

"It's all right," I cup his cheek.

As his blue eyes pierce mine, I wonder why I'm so determined to fight this. Raidyn cares for me in a way no one else ever has. He has tried to keep me safe from the moment he met me. He left his Clan behind for me. Why shouldn't I trust my heart when it tells me that I'm falling in love with this man?

Perhaps this isn't where my crew thought we'd settle, but for some reason, fate brought our ships here. I've never believed in destiny, but as I drop my gaze to Raidyn's chest and I watch the swirling pattern of the bond glow dimly on his scales, I can't deny that this feeling is real.

The way he looks at me with such intense love and devotion, and the warm masculine scent of his body draws me in. I'm tired of fighting this pull I feel toward him.

I stare deep into his eyes and then press my mouth to his. His tongue curls around mine, deepening our kiss.

"Touch me," I whisper against his lips. "I want you to touch me, Raidyn."

As if opening a floodgate, he kisses me like a man possessed. He rolls me beneath him and runs his hand down my body to cup my left breast. A soft moan escapes me as he brushes his thumb over the stiff peak.

I pull back my robes, baring myself entirely to his gaze.

He closes his mouth over my breast and I arch against him, asking for more. His tail curls tightly around my thigh, opening me as he settles between my legs.

I gasp as the hard length of his stav presses insistently

against my folds when he rolls his hips against mine. I want him more than I've ever wanted anyone in my life.

"I can scent your need," he rasps. "Please, allow me to taste you."

Breathless, I nod and he moves down my body. He slicks his tongue between my folds and I cry out as he finds the small bundle of nerves at the top. He growls, low and aroused, concentrating his attention to my sensitive flesh as I run my fingers through his hair, holding him in place while waves of pleasure ripple through me.

I dig my heels into his back, begging him for more. When I've touched myself, it's never felt as amazing as this.

"Raidyn." His name escapes my lips in a breathless moan as he tastes me. "I need you."

He presses one finger into my core and I arch into him, taking him deeper. He pumps in and out of my channel, creating unbearable friction as he continues to tease his tongue through my folds.

He growls again and the sound vibrates straight through me, igniting a fire deep inside. Pleasure roars through my body, so intense all the air rushes from my lungs as I cry out his name.

When I finally come down from my orgasm, he lifts his head to smile at me. I tug on his shoulders to pull him back up my body. I hug him tightly. He places several tender kisses to my face and neck as I run my fingers lazily up and down his back. His hearts hammer against mine and I know he's still aroused and unsated.

I cup his face and meet his eyes. "You didn't climax," I whisper.

He shakes his head. "Your pleasure is all that matters, my mate. I want my first release to be inside you. We will wait until you are ready."

My thighs involuntarily clench at his words as I imagine him thrusting deep in my channel.

He rolls us to the side and pulls me against his chest as he whispers in my ear, "My beautiful mate. You are perfect, my Skye."

CHAPTER 20

SKYE

I don't remember drifting off to sleep, but when I wake, the sun sits high overhead and Raidyn is not in the bed beside me. I stand and pull on my robe, padding downstairs to find him.

His voice in the library catches my attention. Quietly, I move to the doorway to listen. On the screen before him, a dragon-man with dark-gray scales and deep-green eyes is displayed. I recognize his guard, Tai, almost immediately.

"Your father has completely lost his mind. Your cousin is whispering in his ear. They are searching for you. Whatever you do, you must stay hidden."

Raidyn shakes his head. "My father would never hurt me. I know this to be truth."

"Yes, but he is no longer making the decisions. He has left the Clan in Durzain's hands. Your cousin wants you gone so that he may rule in your stead."

Raidyn slams his fist on the table with so much force, the indentation stays after he has lifted his hand. "Durzain is a dishonorable male! How could my father turn our people over to him?"

Tai shakes his head. "Besides you, Durzain is the only family your father has left. And remember, he is not in his right mind."

Raidyn clenches his jaw. "I should have forced him to abdicate long before now, but I did not wish to see him brought low. He was already suffering from the death of my mother."

"What will you do?"

Raidyn runs his hand through his hair. "I must take my mate to find her people. Their ships were downed by Rovaran pirates, who may be still searching Drakaria for them. You know they do not give up their quarry easily."

"Word from the Water Clan is that Varus has already found the humans. He and his warriors brought them to their capital."

"Then I will take my mate there as well. She longs to be reunited with her people."

"It is too dangerous for you to enter Fire Clan territory without—" Tai begins, but Raidyn cuts him off abruptly.

"Varus was like a brother to me once. I believe he will listen to reason."

"You cannot be certain that his people will not attack you."

Raidyn sighs heavily. "I have no choice but to hope he remembers the friendship we once shared. My mate wishes to be reunited with her friend and I must ask a favor of the male I once considered a brother."

Tai frowns. "You cannot mean to take her to them."

"I must." He pauses. "I cannot keep her with me. It is not safe. Not until—"

I step inside. "What are you talking about?"

He spins to face me. "I will take you to the Fire Clan.

They have your crew. It is not safe for you to remain with me. I must challenge my father—my cousin, as well—for the right to rule." He pauses. "I must leave you there. You will not be safe until my father abdicates the throne."

I send him an incredulous look. "And what if something happens to you?"

Instead of answering, he turns back to Tai. "I will contact you later."

Tai bows. "Of course, my prince." He leans forward and shuts off the display. The screen goes dark and then Raidyn reluctantly lifts his gaze to mine.

"I can see no other way to ensure your safety, my mate."

"My mate," I repeat his words. "When you say this, you make us sound like we're already married—*bonded*," I correct myself, using a word he'll understand. "Where I come from, bonded pairs make decisions together. One party doesn't unilaterally decide because they think they know best." Though that's not the whole truth, it's also not a complete lie. Every couple is different, but he doesn't need to know that. Right now, he just needs to understand that I refuse to allow him to make a big decision *for* me instead of *with* me.

Clenching his jaw, he meets my eyes evenly. "I am sorry, but I will not allow you to risk yourself. Gather your things. We are going to the Fire Clan territory."

His tone is commanding. I hold his gaze with narrowed eyes for a moment before I go back upstairs to our room. I have no belongings to gather, except for maybe a spare robe. I'll accompany him to the Fire Clan, but only because I'm desperate to see Lilliana and the rest of our friends again. However, I won't let him leave me there while he goes to wage war against his father and cousin.

He wants me to be his—fine. But I have one condition. When we reach the Fire Clan, I'll tell him I will accept him as my mate, but only if he promises to stay by my side. As desperate as he is to claim me, he'll have to agree.

When I come back downstairs, he studies me warily. He probably expects me to protest more, but instead, I face him calmly. "I'm ready to leave."

CHAPTER 21

RAIDYN

As we make our way to the Fire Clan territory, I pay careful attention to my mate's thoughts and emotions, grateful that I can sense them in this form. Though I've told her I can sense her thoughts, it is clear from the pattern of images that flit through her mind that she does not realize I can visualize them, as well. I probably should have made this clear to her, but I am glad that I did not.

Her mind is a joy to witness.

My hearts soar because she has decided she wants me as her mate. Images of us mating in various positions and places fill her mind. One stands out above all others: She imagines me pressing her against the edge of the bathing pool, her legs wrapped around me as I thrust into her.

This wish I am determined to fulfill when she decides to claim me. Remembering the sweet taste of her nectar on my tongue, I must force myself to focus as I fly us toward the Fire Clan territory.

She wants to claim me as much as I long to claim her but plans to present her decision as a bargaining tool to keep me at her side and safe from danger.

I wish I could stay with her so that we could begin our life right away, but I must deal with my father and cousin. If I do not, she might never be safe. My cousin wants me out of the way so that he can inherit the throne. I must try my best to make her understand that if I had a choice, I would never leave her side.

But in this matter, my resolve is absolute. I will do whatever it takes to make certain she is safe. Even if it costs me my life.

The floating islands give way to mountainous terrain, which in turn fades into an ocean of crimson sand as we enter the Fire Clan territory. I focus my attention away from my mate's thoughts and toward the red plains below. I must remain alert. I have entered enemy territory and do not want to be caught unaware by one of Varus' warriors.

I know we will encounter them sooner or later, but I'd rather avoid them, if possible, for as long as I can. When we meet, I must hope that they will listen to reason before deciding to attack.

Skye must sense my trepidation because she sits up and I realize she, too, is scanning the area for signs of another Drakarian.

I scent one a moment before a deafening roar splits the air—a warning call from a Fire Clan warrior. I recognize him as soon as I scent him on the wind. Rakan, Varus' most trusted guard and faithful friend, has orange-red scales and crimson eyes. I remember him well from my childhood.

He barrels toward us at lightning speed. I cry out to stop him before he attacks. "I have a human female with me!"

Instantly, he slows and hovers beside me, circling once to

verify that I speak truth. As soon as he notices Skye, he calls out to her. "Are you all right?"

"Yes," she shouts over the wind. "We're here to look for my friend, Lilliana, and the rest of my crew."

Rakan's eyes widen slightly. "You speak of our new princess and mate to Prince Varus. She is well and resides in the capital city. We have taken in the rest of your people as well." He narrows his eyes at me. "They are under the protection of the Fire Clan."

"I want to see her," Skye calls. "Will you take us to her?"

He studies me warily for a moment before nodding at Skye. Then he snarls as his crimson eyes meet mine. "No tricks, Warrior of the Wind Clan. Do you understand?"

A low growl escapes me, but I nod in response.

Rakan turns to lead us toward the Fire Clan's capital city. The crimson desert plains give way to a towering plateau. As we climb the cliff face, the orange-and-red layers of rock seem to race by. I can sense Skye's fear of falling through our touch connection.

"Do not worry," I reassure her. "I would never let you fall, my mate."

I cannot help the smile that crests my lips as I sense her complete and total faith in my words.

When we reach the top of the plateau, the altitude affords us a view of the capital city atop the mesa across the river valley below. Turbulent waters feed the canals that line the green farmlands at the base of the mesa. Houses dot the landscape of the valley, but not nearly as many as sit atop the tower of red sand and stone, surrounding a castle at the city center.

The orange-red earthen towers of the palace spiral toward the sky as if reaching for the sun. I squint my eyes as the structure's five golden domes reflect the light in an almost blinding display. Open-air markets emanate enticing, exotic scents that drift across the valley.

Rakan guides us to the central courtyard of the castle. Several Fire Clan guards watch us warily as we land, their eyes widening in shock when they notice Skye.

I transform as soon as my feet touch the ground, quickly wrapping my arms around Skye's waist to lower her the rest of the way.

A sharp cry from inside the large central dome of the palace draws my attention. Before I can comprehend what is happening, Skye rushes from my arms and runs toward Varus' mate—the female with hair the color of flame. This must be Lilliana.

They embrace one another, jumping up and down excitedly in a strange display of greeting.

I growl, matching a low grumble beside me that I quickly realize is coming from Varus. We both watch the interaction warily. Drakarian females are very territorial, known to attack one another in close quarters.

"Is your mate attacking mine?" I grind out.

He arches a brow. "Though it might appear that way, I've learned this is how human females greet one another after spending time apart."

Varus moves to his mate's side and wraps an arm around her waist, tugging her back to him. I notice the permanent glow of the fate mark on his chest; they have completed and sealed their mating. I find intense jealousy flaring to life with my mark. The swirling pattern dims then brightens again, telling the world that Skye and I have yet to seal our bond.

"Why have you come?" Varus demands in a firm voice. His gaze drops to my chest and surprise flits briefly across his expression.

"My mate wanted to be sure that her people were well. I

knew that you had already found them and brought them all here."

He narrows his eyes. "And now that you are here, what will you do?"

"I did not come to fight." With a slight clench of my jaw, I meet his eyes calmly. "I would ask a favor of you."

He tips his head to the side, regarding me with suspicion. "After all this time? What would you ask of me?"

I am glad that he does not deny me outright. Perhaps some part of our friendship still survives in his hearts. As I study him, I am surprised at the realization that it still resides in mine. "I ask you to take care of my mate. To offer her shelter in your lands."

He seems skeptical. "You would leave her with me and my people—your sworn enemies?"

Reluctantly, I nod. "I must."

"But, why would—"

Skye steps forward, and takes my hand firmly in hers. "You're not leaving me here."

With a heavy sigh, I cup her cheek. "It is safer for you to remain here while I—"

"I'm not letting you go," she proclaims. "And that's final."

Varus arches a questioning brow at me. "Perhaps we should discuss this inside."

I nod and we follow him and his mate into the palace. He leads us to a large sitting room that overlooks the back gardens, a verdant space overflowing with plants full of vibrant red, purple, and yellow blossoms. A large fountain with sparkling blue water bubbles in the room's center. The sound of running water relaxes me, lending an air of tranquility to the entire space. The desert breeze blows in through open windows, moving the sheer white curtains like wisps of clouds. We used to spend much time here together, he and I. I remember it all so clearly.

"It's beautiful here," Skye comments, rousing my jealousy once again. I regret that she had no chance to experience the full beauty of my castle because of my father's madness. Although the Fire Clan palace is aesthetically pleasing, it is not nearly as grand or ornate as my home.

Varus turns to us. "I am pleased that you like it." His gaze sweeps to me. "Raidyn, this is my mate, Lilliana. Lilliana, this is my—" he falls silent abruptly as if carefully considering his words before finally concluding, "This is Prince Raidyn of the Wind Clan."

Lilliana smiles kindly. "Varus says you've known each other since you were children. It's nice to meet you."

I'm surprised when she extends her small hand toward me. I look to Skye for direction.

"Our people shake hands when we greet one another," my linaya explains.

Strange that my mate does not mind my touching another female, but I will honor her customs. I reach out and take her smaller hand in mine. She gently shakes it.

Varus' low warning growl beside me tells me he is uncomfortable with this greeting, as well.

"Oh, stop it," Lilliana rolls her eyes at him and I'm surprised when he immediately stops. "It's just a handshake. It's not like I'm asking to claim him or something."

Varus pulls her back to his side and gently nuzzles her hair, murmuring, "Forgive me, my linaya. I am still learning the ways of your people." He turns to me. "Now, tell me. Why would you want to leave your fated here?"

With a heavy sigh, I explain my father's reaction to my human mate and her crew.

Varus narrows his eyes. "If he tries to come for the females, we will be ready for him."

Lilliana glances at her mate in alarm. "You think they would come here and try to take us?"

"I won't let that happen," I reply firmly. "I am returning to the Wind Clan castle to try to reason with my father and convince him to relinquish the throne." I pause. "And if he will not see reason, I must take the Clan from him by force."

Skye tugs at my arm. "No, it's too dangerous. I won't let you go."

"Skye, I have to—"

Alarms suddenly blare throughout the city, the shrill sirens sending a chill down my spine.

Rakan rushes in. "My prince! It is a trap! The Wind Clan is attacking!"

Varus snarls. "How dare you try to deceive me!"

"This was no trick!" I deny. "I spoke truth!"

Instantly, he transforms, his tail whipping out to wrap around my mate and pull her behind him.

How dare he take my mate from my side! I shift into draka form, roaring in anger. "She is mine!"

"You think to bring ruin and destruction upon my people?" he growls.

"If ever you loved me as a brother, know this," I grind out. "I would never betray you like that. I did not deceive you. My cousin Durzain is now controlling my father and wants me gone. He wants the human females too. I'm sure this attack is his doing."

"He's not lying!" Skye cries out. "Listen to him! He's telling you the truth!"

Varus scrutinizes me intently. After a moment, he inclines his head. "I believe you."

Another guard rushes inside. "They're after the humans! They've already taken some from the city!"

Panic fills my veins, for I do not know my cousin's intentions toward the humans if he is willing to steal them away against their will. I have reassured Skye that my people would never harm a female, but Durzain is a dishonorable male. He would not force-mate them, but he might imprison them, only allowing freedom to those who choose a mate among our people.

"Warriors, to me!" Varus commands. I follow him and his guards outside and we take to the skies in our draka forms.

I'm shocked and appalled to find Durzain leading several Wind Clan warriors in an attack on the city. Many of my brethren carry human females on their backs. As the humans wail in terror, I have never felt more ashamed of my people.

CHAPTER 22

RAIDYN

The city is in complete chaos as Drakarian Wind and Fire warriors collide in the air, tearing into flesh with teeth and claws. Obsidian blood rains down onto the city below.

I roar in anger as several of the Wind Clan males, carrying human females on their backs, try to escape by turning to race toward the desert.

"Stop them!" I command Varus' men.

In the distance, I notice Tai and a few other warriors still loyal to me approaching from the north as if pursuing the warriors that are under Durzain's command. They turn as one and rush toward me.

I look to the Fire Clan warriors. "These warriors," I gesture to Tai and the rest, "are loyal to me. Do not attack them."

Blue and aqua scales flash by and I gape as Water Clan warriors join our ranks. Where did they come from? More importantly, on whose side did they come to fight?

As if in answer to my question, a blue male approaches me. Silver eyes meet mine and I immediately recognize Prince Llyr. "We are here to help."

Before I can answer, he shouts an order to his warriors to chase down the Wind Clan males who have taken the human females, then spins back to face me.

"Thank you for your help." My gaze shoots to Durzain. "I will pursue the leader."

Furiously flapping my wings, I rush toward my cousin—now my enemy. "Durzain! Call off this attack before the females are hurt!"

"No!" he snarls. "The humans belong to the Wind Clan."

I watch in horror as one of the Wind warriors spins to avoid an attack from a Water warrior but fails. The Wind warrior roars in pain at the impact while a human female falls from his grip. She releases a feral scream as she tumbles toward the ground with dizzying speed.

Another Wind warrior catches her and she hits his back with a *thud*. As he turns away from the capital, the distraught female yells something incomprehensible and jumps from his back.

Prince Llyr swoops low and catches her just before she hits the ground. I note in dismay that she hangs limply, horribly silent as he races toward the Med Center and the Healers.

Rage boils like fire through my veins as I rush toward Durzain.

Females are being injured. All of this is his fault. It sickens me that a member of my own family is responsible for such a hideous crime.

I barrel into his side, slamming him into a nearby wall. He hits the clay with a sickening *crack*. Recovering quickly, he swipes his claws at me, tearing through one of my sails.

I dig my claws into his flesh and he cries out in pain.

Obsidian blood splatters the buildings around us as we circle and attack, over and over again, until we're falling toward the ground, our claws locked in a deadly embrace.

I twist at the last second, pushing him beneath me so that he takes the brunt of the fall, the *snap* of his bones is a terrible sound. He writhes in agony on the ground.

"Surrender!" I grind out.

"No!"

"As the rightful heir to the throne, I demand your complete surrender! Relent now or I will end you!"

He snarls and rages beneath me. I open my mouth and clamp my teeth around his neck. I do not want to kill him, but I have no choice. I begin to close my jaws and he yelps, "I surrender!"

Releasing my grip, I furiously lift into the air, releasing a bellowing roar. "As your prince and rightful heir to the Wind Clan, I demand that you cease your fighting!"

As one, every warrior turns to face me.

"The Fire Clan is not our enemy! Stand down or you will be executed as traitors to the crown!"

It's a threat I am loath to carry out, but I will if I must. I cannot allow my warriors to take the humans against their will.

"You are better than this!" I cry out, addressing my brethren. "What honor is there in stealing females? For too long, I allowed my father to keep his throne though I knew his rule had been compromised by the death of my mother. But his reign ends this day. We must cease fighting among the Clans. The Gods punished us when they sent the Great Plague, but now, they have seen fit to bless us with compatible females. If we do not stop infighting, we invite punishment from the Gods once more."

I allow my gaze to drift over each warrior of my Clan. "If any of you do not recognize my right to rule our people, speak now and let it be known. I will face and defeat any who dare challenge my claim."

All remain silent. After a moment, one by one, they bow their heads. I turn to my guard and friend, Tai. "Send word to my father and my Clan. Let them know what has happened here this day. Tell them their new king will be returning soon."

He dips his head in a subtle bow. "Yes, my king."

I turn and circle back to Prince Varus. Prince Llyr stands beside him in the palace courtyard. As soon as I land, I transform into my two-legged form and Skye rushes to meet me.

Blood trickles down my body. I'm about to warn her to be gentle, but she wraps her arms around me before I can protest.

"Are you all right?" she asks, worry marring her beautiful features.

I am sore, but I know I will eventually heal, so I lie and assure her that I am alright. Her embrace tightens and I wince before I can catch myself. She releases her grip and stares up at me accusingly. "You're not fine! You're hurt!"

Despite my pain, a small smile quirks my lips at her concern. Was ever a male blessed with a mate as caring as mine? I doubt it.

And yet, when I glance at Varus, I find his mate fussing over him, as well.

He lifts his gaze to mine. "The Earth Clan has been summoned to see to the females." Alarm fills me, but he quickly adds, "Only a few suffered minor injuries after falling from the Wind Clan warriors' grasp. Healer Ranas has told me that all will recover."

I lower my eyes in shame. I cannot believe my Clan is responsible for such a horrible crime. Injuring a female is an offense I would never have thought my people capable of committing.

I am to blame as well; if I had taken the throne when I should have, none of this would have happened.

I scan the city and notice that many structures have sustained damage from the fight. "We will aid in your repairs," I assure Varus.

"That is not necessary," he replies. "But I thank you for the offer, my friend."

Friend. He has not called me this in many cycles. As the word leaves his mouth, my hearts feel whole in a way they have not since my mother's death.

As if sensing my thoughts, he steps forward and claps a hand on my shoulder. "It has been too long since we have seen each other, has it not?"

I grip his shoulder in return and meet his eyes without hesitation. "Yes, it has, my friend."

Tai approaches us, dropping to one knee. "My king, what would you have us do with your cousin?"

I snarl. "He is banished from the Wind Clan and all its territories."

Tai dips his chin in a firm nod. "Yes, my king."

I do not know where my cousin will go. None of the Clans will take him in once word of this attack spreads. Harming a female is a heinous crime to any Clan, and his attempt to steal them will forever mark him as a dishonorable male. He will die without ever taking a mate, for no female will accept a traitor.

As Tai walks away, Skye turns to me, mouth hanging open. Recovering, she bows slightly. "You're the king now?"

I take both her hands and pull her upright. "Never bow to me. You are my mate and my equal. And if you accept, I will make you my queen."

She gives me a hesitant look and then lowers her gaze. "You know, you could probably have any woman you want now that you're the king."

I reach out and stroke her cheek. "Why would I ever want a female besides the one who stands before me?"

A stunning smile curves her mouth. "You still want me?"

"Always."

A tear slips down her cheek. "Then, yes. I will be your queen."

"You will be mine?" I ask, wanting to make certain I've heard her correctly.

"Yes," she repeats. I pull her into my arms, wrapping my wings tightly around her while ignoring the twinge of pain in my muscles. This beautiful, perfect female has agreed to be my mate.

I have never known such happiness.

Healer Ranas approaches me. "My Lord, I can heal you if you'd like."

A low growl rumbles in my throat as he interrupts this perfect moment between me and my mate.

Skye snaps, "Don't growl at him. You're injured. Let him heal you."

Immediately, I fall silent. My female is fierce when she does not get her way, so I refuse to argue with her.

Ranas' healing fire spreads like a soothing balm over my many injuries. I release a deep sigh of relief as I watch the tissues of my wing folds begin to knit back together.

A bellowing roar draws my attention to the north and I look to the sky to see my father flying toward me, two of his guards in tow.

"What is—" Varus starts to ask, but I interrupt him.

"Watch over my mate," I call over my shoulder as I shift into draka form to intercept my father. I worry that he's come to finish what Durzain could not. As angry as I am, I do not wish to fight the male who raised me.

I meet him in midair. "What is the meaning of this?" I shout.

"My son," he answers, moving closer.

I release a warning snarl. "I cannot believe you are responsible for the dishonorable actions that occurred here today."

"Forgive me." His voice is laced with regret. "Once I found out what Durzain had planned, I came as fast as I could to stop him."

I narrow my eyes. "And why should I believe you? You were the one who ordered my mate imprisoned."

He lowers his head in shame. "I was wrong, my son. I know that now. I knew it the moment you left the castle."

"I defeated Durzain and have exiled him from our lands," I state firmly. "And now, I demand that you give up the throne. You are not fit to rule; you haven't been since Mother died."

A tear slips down his cheek. "Take the throne. It is yours. Exile me if you must, but know this: I realized my error as soon as you left. Durzain promised to help us reunite once I found you. It was only recently that I learned he meant to kill you so he could inherit the throne."

Tai falls in line beside me. "It is truth, my king. He was deceived by Durzain."

"Forgive me, Raidyn. I have been a terrible father to you ever since your mother died. You remind me so much of her... it is difficult to look upon you without fear that I may lose you as well." He pauses to regain control of his voice. "In my fear, I only succeeded in pushing you away, and for that, I am sorry."

"It will be difficult to repair all the damage you have caused, Father." I pause. "But the blame lies with me, too. I should have taken the throne long ago when I first realized you were broken beyond recovery by Mother's death."

"Please, Raidyn. Tell me how we can remedy this rift between us."

Clenching my jaw, I lower my gaze. In truth, I do not know how to close this gap. "For now, I must concentrate on returning order and stability to our kingdom. Return home and we will discuss this when I get back. But first, I must see to my mate and make peace with the other Clans."

He bows his head. "Of course, my son."

With that, he banks to head back to our territory, while I spin to return to my mate.

I find her standing next to Varus and Lilliana, anxiously fidgeting as I land before her. I shift back into my two-legged form and wrap a possessive arm around her waist, pleased when she wraps an arm around me in return.

I face Varus. "I would like to pursue an alliance with all the Clans. But first, I must return to my people and restore some semblance of order. I do not know what damage Durzain's rule has caused."

Varus nods. "Of course."

Skye moves off to speak with Varus' mate, Lilliana, leaving he and I alone. For many cycles, I have harbored anger at the Fire Clan and Varus over the death of my mother. My mate made me realize it was not their fault she died. My mother chose to sacrifice herself so that I could be saved. In my grief and my pain, I wrongly blamed Varus and his kin for her death.

He and I used to be as close as brothers. After so many cycles, I do not even know where to begin to restore the relationship between us.

As if sensing my troubled thoughts, Varus extends his arm. I clasp my hand around his forearm and he does the same to me in return.

I meet his eyes evenly. "It has been a long time, Varus. I do not know how best to repair our broken relationship, but I know I would like to try."

"I agree," he replies. "It has been too long and I have missed you, brother."

His words touch me deeply. Emotions lodge in my throat but I manage to speak around them. "Forgive me for all the offenses I have laid against you."

A smile tugs at his lips. "They are already forgiven." His gaze drifts to our mates, talking with one another off to the side. "You are both welcome to visit anytime you wish."

"Thank you. We will return as soon as we can to discuss plans for a treaty between our Clans."

CHAPTER 23

SKYE

Night has fallen by the time we arrive in Wind Clan territory. Lights from the capital below cast a soft glow over the surface of the floating island. Its beauty takes my breath away. Gray-and-white stone buildings proudly encircle the castle. Tall, majestic towers reach for the clouds and a waterfall drops off the side of the gardens onto a smaller island directly below.

We land on a large balcony on the closest tower and Tai lands beside us. He turns to face Raidyn. "Your father has left for his private estate. The castle is entirely yours, my King." He bows. "The staff report that the royal wing is still being cleared out for your arrival."

"This room will do," Raidyn assures him.

Tai bows again and takes off from the balcony, landing in the large courtyard with the rest of the guards below. As one, they all look up and bow. Raidyn dips his chin in a subtle acknowledgment and then turns back to me with a heated look in his eyes.

I release a surprised laugh as he scoops me up in his arms without warning and carries me into the room. I smile as I recognize my surroundings immediately. "This is your room, isn't it? We stayed here before."

"Yes."

"I'm glad," I tell him as I wrap my arms around his neck.

He looks curious. "Why is that?"

I smile. "Because we never got to use the bed last time."

His jaw drops before his eyes light with joy. He crushes his lips to mine in a searing kiss and I return it with equal fervor.

He pulls back and his nostrils flare. "I scent your need, my mate, and I long to claim you as mine. Do you desire me to be yours?"

"Yes." I reach out to caress his face. "But there's something I need to tell you first."

His smile fades, replaced by a look of concern. "What is it?"

"I talked with Lilliana. Healer Ranas told her that she's with child already." His lips part as he stares down at me. Though he said his people are desperate for children, we've never talked about whether the two of us want kids. I need to know. "So if we make love, there's a chance we might—"

He cuts off my words with a passionate kiss as he purrs, "I desire nothing more than to have a fledgling with you. To fill you with my seed and let it take root deep in your womb." He presses his forehead to mine. "I swear I will guard our egg with my life. I will be a good mate to you and—"

"Egg?" I sputter. "What are you talking about?"

He tips his head to the side. "Humans do not lay eggs?"

I shake my head as I gape. "No. We carry our babies to term."

He swallows thickly. "It is safe for you, my mate?"

Just hearing him call me his mate with concern lacing his

voice melts my heart. I nod. "Lots of women have babies, Raidyn. But what if I get pregnant sooner rather than later? I mean, I don't know what kind of precautions we could take if you want to wait. Healer Ranas wasn't sure either, though he offered to try to develop some birth control if we need it."

He shakes his head, tenderly stroking my cheek. "I want to make a life with you and create a family together. It would be..." His eyes brighten with tears. "It is a dream I never imagined could be mine until I found you." He pauses, lowering his gaze. "You truly do not care about my scar?"

"I love you, Raidyn. Your scar is a part of you, and I love every part. Do you care that I don't have wings, scales, claws, or fangs?" I tease.

He beams. "Your lack of natural defenses does rouse my protective instincts, but it does not make me love you any less." He takes my hand and places it on his chest, directly over the swirling fate bond pattern. "You are my hearts, Skye. I love you."

Hugging me tightly to his chest, he walks us into the cleansing room. He sets my feet on the floor then carefully pulls off my robe, allowing the fabric to drop to the floor. He leads me into the bathing pool, pressing a hidden glowing panel nearby. Tiles rise from the floor of one edge and water streams down into the main pool like a tiny waterfall.

I smile. "What is this?"

"Remember, when I am in draka form, I can sense your thoughts." Gently, he pulls me into the water with him. "I caught your fantasy of us making love beneath the waterfall; it was one of my favorites." A slow smile curves his mouth. "I want to take you just as you imagined I would for our first mating, my linaya."

My jaw drops. "You caught all of that?" My entire body flushes with warmth, both in embarrassment and arousal.

His nostrils flare and his blue, vertically slit pupils

contract and expand as he rasps, "You are not as upset as you pretend. I can scent your desire."

"That's not fair," I try but fail to suppress a grin. "I have every right to be mad at you for keeping that from me. I thought you could only sense the words in my mind, not images."

He gathers me in his arms, pulling me against the hard muscles of his chest as his tail snakes up my thigh. A soft moan escapes me as the tip glides through my already slick folds. "Your body is telling me that you are not mad. In fact," he grabs my backside and hauls me up against him, "it is telling me something else."

His stav is a hard bar between us, so dangerously close to where I need him most. I wrap my legs around him then reach between us to stroke his length. His mouth falls open as a low groan escapes him.

Gently, he pulls away.

I open my mouth to protest but he captures my lips with his. His tongue curls around mine to deepen our kiss, stealing the breath from my lungs. He cups my left breast and I push into his hand, wanting more. He kisses a heated trail from my jaw to the curve of my neck and shoulder, then closes his mouth over my breast, laving at the peak until it hardens to a bead.

He uses his tongue to drive my desire even higher.

I run my fingers through his hair, holding him in place. He turns his attention to my other breast as his tail teases the sensitive flesh of my folds.

I moan. "Please, Raidyn, I want more. I need you."

He groans as I wrap my hand around his stav. He's so large, my fingers don't meet while wrapped around him. I run my thumb across the tip and he growls low in arousal. He rips his mouth from my breast and then hauls me up against him. His tail wraps firmly around my thigh as he parts my legs and fits himself between them.

The crown of his stav bumps my entrance and I gasp.

He stares down at me with a fiery and possessive gaze. "I need you," he rasps. "Tell me you are mine."

"I'm yours," I barely manage, breathless with desire.

His eyes hold mine as he slowly pushes into me. The slight sting as my body stretches to accommodate him is nothing compared to the delicious friction of his thick, ridged shaft. I close my eyes and moan his name as he rocks his hips back and forth, pushing deeper with each movement until he's completely seated inside me.

Panting heavily, he stares deep into my eyes. "So tight," he rasps, clenching his jaw.

"Feels so good." My voice is a breathless whisper as he begins long, deep strokes inside me.

I run my hands down his back, tracing the thick planes of muscle as they flex beneath my fingers with each thrust of his body into mine. He presses me against the wall of the pool and captures my lips in a branding kiss as each thrust grows deeper and more forceful.

I close my eyes, completely lost in sensation. He grips my chin firmly, causing my eyes to open again, seeing his ice-blue gaze meet mine. "I want to watch you as you reach your release."

Heat builds at my core as the thick ridges of his stav move within me, rubbing my inner walls in all the right ways. I dig my nails into his back. His rhythm is relentless; he is just as intense when he makes love as he is when proclaiming that I'm his and always have been, from the moment he met me.

"You are my mate," he growls possessively.

A burst of heat deep in my core makes me gasp. "What was that?" I barely manage.

"My precum to soften your womb to receive my seed," he

grinds out, his intense gaze holding mine. "I will fill you many times this night, my beautiful linaya."

With his chest pressed to mine, his growl vibrates my skin, sending ripples of pleasure through my veins. The small muscles of my channel quiver and flex around his length. I throw my head back and cry out his name as my release overwhelms me.

His stav pulses and he roars my name as he erupts deep inside my core, flooding me with a delicious warmth. It feels like it goes on forever, igniting another orgasm. Wave after wave of pleasure moves through me as he fills me with his seed.

He drops his head to the curve of my neck and shoulder, both of us panting heavily as we grip one another. I lock my legs around him, unwilling to separate just yet.

He lifts his gaze to me. "You want me again so soon?" he asks as he thrusts his hips against mine.

"You mean you don't need to rest before we—"

He shakes his head and once again begins to stroke in a languorous rhythm. I throw my head back and breathe his name, enjoying the renewed sensation of his ridged stav.

His breath warms my ear as he rasps, "I'm going to take you all night, my beautiful mate. Filling you over and over again so that every male within twenty arcums will be able to scent that you are mine."

The breath stutters from my lungs at his erotic words as his hips flex into me.

This is by far better than anything I've ever read in a romance novel or could have ever imagined.

EPILOGUE

SKYE

R aidyn blinks down at me, his brow furrowed deeply. "What do you mean, you need dresses?"

"Are you telling me that Drakarian women only wear robes?" I look down my body at the green robe I currently have on.

It's comfortable, but I was kind of hoping for something more elaborate. I've always fantasized about wearing a gown fit for a princess and dancing at a ball—all those things I've read about in romance novels. Though I know it's silly, I can't help but want the fairytale.

"Why wouldn't they?" he asks. "We have wings. It would not be easy for a Drakarian to wear what you are describing."

I reach up and cup his cheek. "That's all right. I don't need a dress. It was just a silly fantasy, anyway." I shrug. "I'm happy with you and that's all that matters. So, whatever your people would normally do at these peace celebrations is what we'll do."

His eyes flare with heat. "It is your... fantasy to wear a dress?"

I grin. Ever since he read my thoughts and saw my dreams of making love in various places and positions, we've tried them all. He loves fulfilling my fantasies.

"Yes. We never wore them on the ship because they're not exactly practical and we never had any occasion to dress up. But I always dreamed of wearing a gown to a big, fancy ball. And I always imagined a handsome prince tearing it from my body at the end of the night to make passionate love to me," I add because I know he won't be able to resist that.

He pulls me close as a low growl of arousal vibrates deep in his chest.

Raidyn thought it was strange at first that humans wear clothes all the time, but I've insisted. We have compromised on sleepwear, however; I gave up trying to wear pajamas since he ends up tearing them off me when he comes to bed anyway. It's not quite the sacrifice that I teased him it would be.

He is insatiable, my dragon mate—but then again, so am I.

He cups my chin, leaning in to press a tender kiss to my lips. His blue eyes pierce mine. "If it is that important to you, then I will talk it over with Varus. We will see that the tailors fit each human who so desires with a dress."

A bright smile lights my face. "Really?"

"You already know I would do anything you desire, my beautiful mate." He smiles and places a hand low on my abdomen.

My period is late, but then again, I suppose it's to be expected. We make love two or three times a day, sometimes more.

He leans in and gently skims the tip of his nose along mine before moving down to the curve of my neck. Inhaling deeply, he growls low in his throat. "Your scent is stronger now," he rasps. "I am certain you carry our child."

When he pulls back, I run my fingers through the hair at the nape of his neck and stare deep into his gorgeous blue eyes. "And does that make you happy?"

"More than words can say," he whispers against my lips.

ABOUT ARIA WINTER

Aria Winter

For information about upcoming releases Like me on Facebook (www.facebook.com/ariawinterauthor) or sign up for upcoming release alerts at my website:

Ariawinter.com

Other books from Aria coming soon:
Elemental Dragon Warriors Series
Claimed by the Fire Dragon Prince
Stolen by the Wind Dragon Prince
Rescued by the Water Dragon Prince
Healed by the Earth Dragon Prince
Once Upon A Fairy Tale Romance Series
Taken by the Dragon: A Beauty and the Beast Retelling
Captivated by the Fae: A Cinderella Retelling

Rescued By The Merman: A Little Mermaid Retelling

Once Upon a Shifter Series
Ella and her Shifters

ABOUT JADE WALTZ

Jade Waltz lives in Illinois with her husband, two sons, and her three crazy cats. She loves knitting, playing video games, and watching Esports. Jade's passions include the arts, green tea and mints — all while writing and teaching marching band drill in the fall.

Jade has always been an avid reader of the fantasy, paranormal and sci-fi genres and wanted to create worlds she always wanted to read.

She writes character driven romances within detailed universes, where happily-ever-afters happen for those who dare love the abnormal and the unknown. Their love may not be easy—but it is well worth it in the end.

Website: www.jadewaltz.com
    Facebook Group: Jade Waltz Literary Alcove
    Twitter: @authorjadewaltz
    Instagram: @authorjadewaltz
    Email: authorjadewaltz@gmail.com

Also By Jade Waltz:

Solo Works:

Project Universe Timeline:

Project: Adapt #1 – Found
 Project: Adapt #2 – Achieve
 Project: Adapt #3 – Develop

Project: F5 #1 – Bird of Prey
 Project: F5 #2 – Scaled Heart